On Grove Street

A Novella

Second Edition

Marc Mayfield

Paperback ISBN: 979-8-218-29968-2
Ebook ISBN: 979-8-218-29969-9
Library of Congress Control Number: 2023920231

Interior design and typesetting by Jess LaGreca, Mayfly Design
Original cover design by Laura Rose
First Printing, 2023
Printed in the United States of America

On Grove Street is a work of fiction.
Similarities of the characters to persons living
and dead are unintentional.
To the best of the author's knowledge there is no
Grove Street in Santa Rosa, California.

For Gayle, without whom . . .

Also by Marc Mayfield
In The Driver's Seat: Interstate Trucking, a Journey
Sam and Other Dogs

The mind is its own place, and in itself
Can make a heav'n of hell, a hell of heav'n.
John Milton

1

San Francisco, Mission and 1st Streets, May 15, 1991.

In the last minute of his life Ian Christian Hamilton, Esq. walks arm in arm along a crowded sidewalk with his secretary, Mindy Baker. He thinks about the evening ahead. After a steak dinner and two drinks she'll do anything in bed. Anything.

She says, "Ian, we need to talk. I'm . . ."

"Come on! We can make the light if we hurry."

"We need to talk about . . ."

"We can talk tomorrow. Now what did I tell you? We missed it and we have to wait. You know I don't like that."

The light changes. He hesitates and says, "Remind me to . . ."

A silent bullet shatters his left eye then tears away half of his face and the back of his skull. Mindy Baker is sprayed with blood and brains. Cranial splinters lodge in her cheek, where they will leave scars. Hamilton is knocked backwards. A second bullet bores through his heart, shocks his body, and flattens against the pavement, rippling a pool of blood beneath him. Mindy Baker begins to scream.

Inspector Joe D'Alessandro, San Francisco Police Department, sighed and lifted a blanket off Ian Hamilton's body. It's too bad, he thought. Life isn't fair. Here he was, weeks from mandatory retirement, Mr. Hamilton's very public demise promised the most interesting casework in years, and someone else would have the pleasure of solving the crime if it didn't go cold. What would he do on the first morning he didn't have to go into the office, or the next, or the next? Go fishing? He sighed again and lowered the blanket.

He said, "Keep the gawkers away, Sergeant. Did anyone see or hear anything?"

"No one that we've talked to, not even Ms. Baker."

"Keep asking. Somebody always knows something."

"Dead before he hit the concrete. Why the second shot?"

"Making sure. Or just because."

"This'll be a tough one."

"Not really. All we have to do is find the person or persons who helped Mr. Hamilton expire. I'd like to talk to the ... uh ... secretary when the medics are finished with her."

"Ms. Baker," D'Alessandro said, "I know this is difficult, but ..."

"I was trying to tell him."

"Ma'am?"

"That ..."

"Ms. Baker? I'm listening."

"That I'm pregnant again, I wasn't going to have a second abortion, and we'd have to get married soon, like he promised. Now I suppose it's too late. He's really dead, isn't he?"

"Yes, ma'am. I'm afraid he is."

"He was never going to marry me."

Two days later. The home of Edward Hayes, Sonoma, California.

Nine-year-old Debbie Sweetman is on time for her weekly music lesson. She carries her guitar and homework to Mr. Hayes' front door, which is open, as it always is. She rings the bell like she always does and knows that Mr. Hayes will call for her to come in. Then Sandy, Mr. Hayes' Golden Retriever, will bark and run to greet her. But not today. There is a strange smell in the house and Sandy is quiet. She turns toward her father, who waits beside his car.

"Debbie, what's wrong?"

She stands, trembling, and says nothing.

"Honey, stay there."

Mr. Sweetman walks through the living room and down a hallway. In the recording studio, he sees Edward Hayes' prized Martin guitar smashed to bits. He sees a bloodstained wall and Sandy cowering beside a slippered foot. He knows that Edward Hayes is on the floor behind his desk. He knows that Edward Hayes is dead.

Sonoma County Sheriff's Deputy Ben Hyatt ducked under the barrier tape and walked through the open door at the Hayes house. Two evidence technicians—men he trusted, men he knew as friends—were already at work. One said, "Shot in the head and chest, Ben. No casings. Doesn't look like a burglary. No forced entry, no sign of a struggle. There's just the body and a busted guitar."

"Somebody was angry about something. How long ago?"

"I'm guessing he'd been dead two hours when Mr. Sweetman found him, so it happened at noon, give or take a few minutes. Left a mess, nothing we haven't seen before, it's only blood."

Blood. A coagulated pond on the floor under Hayes' chair. Spatter patterns on the wall behind him and, on his desk, across the front page of a two-day old *San Francisco Chronicle*.

"Looks like Ian Hamilton died without even knowing it," said the other technician. "But Hayes knew. He was probably facing his killer. Nice studio, by the way. Soundboard, guitars, amps, gold and platinum records on the wall. I know those songs. He wrote them?"

Hyatt knew the songs, too. Who didn't? You couldn't buy groceries or go into a department store without hearing them. "Apparently," he said. "I'm going to nose around the house."

Living room. One bedroom. One full bathroom. A half-bath. Compact gourmet kitchen. Tiffany lamps, antique furniture, hardwood floors, Persian carpets. Framed artwork, probably original, maybe even commissioned. Nothing disturbed, dresser drawers all closed. No, it didn't look like a burglary. The Golden Retriever followed him from room to room. "Good girl," he said. He looked at her dog tag. "Let's find you a home, Sandy."

One of the technicians said, "Sweetman told me his daughter loves her."

"Okay, let's ask him."

"Hayes kept personal journals, Ben. There's a whole cabinet full, bound notebooks all the way back to 1966. One for each year."

The journals of Edward Hayes. Blue ink on white, lined paper. Neat, angular handwriting. Ticket stubs. Newspaper clippings. Letters. Hyatt pulled out four volumes and quickly thumbed through them. There would be time later on to read carefully and take notes.

January 1, 1966
17 years old today. I will assemble my life carefully and move forward. Who shall I be?

January 28, 1966
Do not understand why I don't have any friends.

February 14, 1966
No longer a virgin! It happened in my room with Ronald!

August 23, 1967
Drove up to Sonoma County for college . . . Will start out living in a dorm to meet people and make some friends.

October 6, 1968
Played and sang at Lefty's Bar & Grill. Lots of applause for me!

December 8, 1968
What do I have to do? Still have no friends.

August 25, 1969
Moved into the house with Ian Hamilton . . . Address is 805 Grove Street, Santa Rosa. Next week we start interviews for a roommate.

At his desk three days later, Hyatt checked the Monday morning newspapers. *The Press Democrat* led with Hamilton and placed Hayes on page 2. The *San Francisco Chronicle* continued its front-page coverage of the Hamilton murder.

> Police believe Ian Hamilton was shot from a warehouse across the street, but have released no other details. Bystanders did not hear gunshots. Anyone with information is asked to call Inspector Joe D'Alessandro, San Francisco Police Department.

Hyatt sat through roll call, then he conferred with his boss, Sheriff Robert Olson.

"Joe's a crusty old-timer," Olson said. "Got out of the bullpen years ago. They gave him his own office at SFPD Headquarters and he swore he'd never share it with anyone. It's known as Joe's Cave. You'll be lucky if he listens to you at first, but call him anyway. Tell him I said hello. That should soften him up. It's fine by me if you want to work with him, so tell him that, too. Here's his phone number."

———————

Joe D'Alessandro bit into a donut and let his phone ring. The caller was probably another whackjob who would claim that he'd killed Ian Hamilton with a death ray or that he knew the killer's identity and how big was the reward? He'd answered eight kook calls since the story broke. There'd be more. But as his father used to say, you take things as they come, like the weather. Through the donut he said, "Yeah?"

"Inspector D'Alessandro?"

"Who wants to know?"

"Ben Hyatt, Sonoma County Sheriff's Office. Sheriff Olson sends his regards. He suggested I call you."

"Why?"

"I'm working a fresh homicide. My deceased and Ian Hamilton were roommates twenty-two years ago. Maybe somebody killed both of them. Maybe you and I are looking for the same somebody."

"I'm listening."

2

Joe's Cave. A small, windowless office lit by a single desk lamp. Government-green ceiling and walls. Black linoleum floor, scuffed and worn thin. One battered desk and one battered chair. Cardboard file boxes stacked four high.

A heavy-set man sat behind the desk, tie loosened, shirt unbuttoned at the collar, jacket thrown over the back of a chair, reading. Hyatt rapped on the door frame. The heavy man closed a thick manila folder, stretched a rubber band around the ends, dropped it into a cardboard box and said, "Cold cases. There's never a shortage."

Hyatt said, "Inspector D'Alessandro?"

"Maybe."

"Ben Hyatt."

"I know. Bob Olson called me. Sit."

Hyatt pointed to a framed photograph on D'Alessandro's desk. "Family member?"

"My father, the day he made captain. He was killed responding to a domestic two weeks after that. The wife shot him. Poppa never wanted to do anything but police work."

"Same here."

"Same here. You married?"

"Not anymore. Why?"

"Just curious. Girlfriends?"

"None at the moment."

"Veteran?"

"Army. Vietnam. Infantry."

"Army. Korea. Infantry. Where do you live?"

"Near Petaluma."

"On a chicken ranch?"

"Yep. In a converted barn."

"Let's go down to Jake's deli. I'll lose my edge if I don't catch some of his potato salad and a pastrami on rye."

"There's one thing, Inspector . . ."

"Joe. That's what people call me when they're not mad at me. Tell me the one thing later."

At Jake's, Joe held the door open for Hyatt, called out, "Hey, Jake," waved two fingers, and led the way to a table in a far corner. A server brought iced Buds and a platter of hot pastrami, wafer-thin and piled high between slices of fragrant rye bread. And potato salad.

Joe said, "Dig in," and waited. "What do you think?"

"It's good. I'd bring a date here."

"Jake bakes his own bread. His donuts are the best in the city. Okay, Ben. Where are we?"

"Two former roommates were murdered two days apart. That can't be a coincidence."

"You saw the newspapers. We've asked anyone with information to contact us. No one has. I didn't put it in the press release, but I think there was only one shooter."

"Edward Hayes was shot inside his house, close-up, through the left eye and in the heart. Probably one shooter, probably 9mm. Hamilton?"

"Left eye and heart, probably .45 ACP."

"But not at close range. Can you think of a rifle chambered in .45 Auto?"

"Not offhand."

"Neither can I. No audible gunshots?"

"That's the easy part. Hamilton wasn't the first man killed with a suppressed weapon."

"There's still that one thing."

"And it is?"

"I'm cleared to work with you on this. I hope that's okay."

"Come for dinner tonight. If my better half approves, you're in."

Ben reached for the check but it was already in Joe's hand.

"Not fast enough, deputy. Here's our address. Dinner goes on the table at 6 p.m. sharp. Don't be late."

Joe came to the door with a smile, two glasses of wine, and a key. "You are about to enjoy the best lasagna and cannoli in the world, and you'll need a place to stay when you're in town. We've a spare bedroom downstairs. Private entrance. Rose, this is Ben Hyatt. Ben, Rose, my wonderful wife. She really is my better half."

Rose said, "Hi, Ben. We want you to make yourself at home."

"I think this is pretty good Chianti," Joe said. "What do you think?"

After dinner Ben said, "Rose, Joe was right. That is the best lasagna in the world."

"Thank you, Ben. You two talk in the living room. I'll clean up."

Ben said, "Why homicide investigations, Joe?"

"Less complicated than the vice squad, which I worked for three years. Child prostitutes in Chinatown's brothels, pimped teenagers sharing needles south of Market, working girls and working boys in the Tenderloin, cops looking the other way, cops on the take. I cared too much. Couldn't adjust to things as they were."

"Joe hated it," Rose said from the kitchen. "More cannoli, Ben?"

"Well, they're delicious, but I . . ."

"Go ahead," Joe said. "You know you want to. You went to college. What did you study?"

"I started with criminal justice, drifted into architecture and psychology, and finished in CJ with a minor in English Literature. Even wrote a crime novel."

"Any good?"

"Hell no it wasn't any good. Thank you, Rose."

"You're welcome. And you, Ben. What made you choose criminology?"

"I'm interested in justice and why people do what they do."

"Those were my father's reasons," Joe said. "He enjoyed casework and so do I. I'm always looking for the loose ends."

"Discovery. Details. All the puzzle pieces. The whole story. On my own dime if I have to."

"That's good. 'The whole story.' Are you religious?"

"Couldn't do the job if I was. Every day would be a failed test of my faith. You?"

"No. I've learned to leave people alone in the belief department, but I always ask my partners so I won't offend. I was an altar boy until our priest put a hand on my leg. I ran home and told my father. He gave the priest a bloody nose. After that, we weren't Catholics or believers. No more parochial school for me and my brother. Poppa enrolled us at Marina Junior High, which was better. There were girls, and there was Rose."

They talked until Joe said, "Well, it's late and I have to get my beauty sleep. I'll show you your room. New bed, clean sheets, bathroom, clean towels, books if you want to stay up and read."

"This is very kind of you and Rose. Thank you."

"I get up early. I'll see you downtown."

Joe closed the bedroom door and Ben heard Rose say, "You were right. I do like him. He's a lot like Anthony."

Joe's Cave. Two desks. Two chairs. An extra lamp. No boxes, no folders.

Ben said, "And the cold-case files are . . .?"

"At someone else's workstation so I won't have to think about them. I've been meaning to clear them out. This desk is yours. We've ordered a phone for you. If you need anything, just ask."

"How do you want to start?"

"It'll take a day to line up a car assignment. You won't need to run around on your own dime. You already know how to get to Jake's. That's very important. I'll show you where the coffee pot is and introduce you to a few people, then we should visit the scene of the crime, as they say in the movies. I'll drive."

"Hamilton died here," Joe said. "I think the shots came from the roof of that warehouse across the street, which, by the way, was owned by his father and, after the old man died, by our very own Ian Hamilton. We'll probably have to break in."

Joe wedged a crowbar against a padlock and pulled down hard. The lock snapped.

"Perfect," Ben said. He shouldered a sliding steel door back along its rail. "Whew. What died in there?"

"Old buildings always stink. Let's leave it open. I'll call for a unit to guard the door while we're inside. Any lights? Is there an electrical panel or something?"

"Yeah. Ceiling fans too. I hear a ventilation system."

"We'll have to wait for the unit."

They watched a young woman jaywalk, then angle toward them. High heels, coy glances, prominent Adam's apple.

Joe said, "When I was in Vice I used to ask them, 'Is this what you want to do with your life? What about school, a career, a profession?' It was like talking to the wall most of the time. But some streetwalkers are intelligent. You can have a real conversation with them." He flashed his badge, said, "Please keep moving," and shook his head. "I don't get it, Ben."

"Get what?"

"Men with men, even if they look like women."

"Live and let live, I say."

"Oh, I agree. Now. I didn't always see things that way. When I was young, I was very moralistic. I knew everything and everything was black or white. Now, like my hair, everything is shades of gray. Our youngest, Alex, is gay. That was not at first easy to deal with, though Rose and I never loved him any less. He's a damn good lawyer. But I still don't *get* it."

"And your other sons?"

"Jay—the middle one—is happily married with two kids. He's in something called IT. Information Technology. I have no idea what that is."

"What does the oldest do?"

"We lost Anthony in Vietnam. Ah, here's the unit. Let's find the shooter's hide."

Dim light, cobwebs, dust on every surface, the air a brown haze stirred by the ventilators. All across the first floor 1930s cars and trucks were parked side by side and end to end. They sagged against each other on flat tires or sat level on wood blocks, fenders rusted through, faded lettering on the doors: *Hamilton Moving and Storage.* In an alcove, cardboard boxes shielded two burned cars from view and canvas tarps covered a truck, its cab a sieve of bullet holes.

Ben said, "Is that blood on the seat?"

"It was, 60 years ago."

"Well, I guess we should get on up to the roof."

"There's a freight elevator. Let's see if it works."

On the roof Ben said, "Not from here. Too open."

"Right. Anyone in a nearby high-rise could have seen him."

On the fourth floor they found old furniture, Tiffany lamps, rotting Persian carpets, and an open gun case.

Joe said, "Whoa. Beretta over-and-under. Twelve gauge, figured wood, engraved receiver. Both barrels loaded, let's fix that. And here we have a Beretta invoice from June 1950 for one just like it, with a consecutive serial number."

"A matched pair."

"So, where's the other gun?"

"Look at these, Joe."

Footprints led to a fire door that had been jimmied open and left partly closed.

"That's how he got in," Ben and Joe said together then laughed together. They followed the footprints through a maze of shipping crates to windows that offered a clear view of the sidewalk where Ian Hamilton died.

"No sole marks," Ben said. "Like he was only wearing socks."

"Disposable surgeon's booties. Had an amateur perp do that once, so I couldn't track his size-14 shoes. He thought. But our guy is a professional, maybe ex-military. Maybe he was a sniper. We won't find a cartridge, a fiber from his shirt, or a hair off his head. Probably a waste of time to hunt for prints. I'll get the forensic people to come over anyway."

"These windows were painted shut years ago."

"He only had to open one."

"And not even all the way."

"Here. He cut through the paint."

"Laid a tarp on the floor."

"Sat on a camp stool."

"Opened his duffle, placed a bean bag shooting rest on the sill."

"A click or two and he was sighted in."

"Did his shooter-get-ready thing and waited for Hamilton."

"But not too long."

"No. He knew where Hamilton would be, and when."

"Two quick shots. He was good enough not to hit anyone else."

"He closed the window."

"Put his gear back in the duffle and . . ."

"Checked twice to make sure he didn't leave anything behind."

"Put on a pair of gloves. Walked back to the fire door. Climbed down the fire escape to the alley."

"Took off his gloves and booties."

"And his hair net."

"Carefully put everything in plastic trash bags."

"Tossed the bags into his car, van, truck, whatever."

"And drove or was driven away."

"The question is why."

"And who."

"And for whom."

"Let's move on to Hamilton's office."

Tall arch-top windows opened onto Mission Street and a view of the Hamilton warehouse. Leather executive chair behind a mahogany desk. Mahogany conference table. Law journals on mahogany shelves. Persian carpets. Pens and legal pads scattered about. Messages on the answering machine, a woman's voice. "Please call me." "Please call me." "Please call me. I'm still your wife." Four bankers boxes—*Charbonneau v. Hamilton*. Two work tables all but hidden by briefs, court orders, depositions, and reports from private investigators. Framed photographs arranged on a teak sideboard: Ian Hamilton beneath the Eiffel Tower. At the wheel of a sailboat. Holding a tennis racquet. Next to an elephant he'd shot on safari. Seated in one Porsche after another.

Joe said, "You'd think there would be a picture of him *with* someone."

"There is." Ben picked up a sepia photograph in a tarnished frame: four young people—three men and a woman—on the front porch of an old house. Two of the men cradled acoustic guitars and sat upright on straight-back chairs. The woman stood between them, closer to one than the other. Ian Hamilton sat by the stoop, relaxed and easy, a shotgun across his lap.

Joe said, "Who do we have here?"

"I think that one's Edward Hayes."

"Are the others Hamilton and Hayes' roommates?"

"More than roommates. Look how she's pressing against him."

"What about the gun?"

"A prop. Lunch at Jake's?"

"Yeah, let's eat. Wait . . . look at this profile of Hamilton. *San Francisco Chronicle*. Society pages."

Ian Hamilton — Still The Same

Well-known Bay Area divorce attorney . . . popular on Marin County tennis courts . . . former president of the Sausalito Yacht Club . . . exercise enthusiast. "I weigh what I weighed in college. In more ways than one, I'm still the same."

Married three times, Mr. Hamilton inherited a San Francisco warehouse and an office building across the street, where his law office is located. "I run my little empire from here." He swivels in his executive chair and twirls a tennis racquet. "On the court or in court, I play fair, but I play hard. I don't like to lose. My father raised his boy to be a winner."

Rain or shine, after work Mr. Hamilton walks a brisk half-mile to the ferry that takes him to Sausalito, where he climbs Excelsior Lane to the hillside apartment building he owns, and his penthouse. "I'm a creature of habit," he says. "I leave my office every afternoon at exactly 4:45. I time the traffic lights so I won't have to stop."

Joe said, "Anyone reading that would know when and where to find Ian Hamilton."

3

After lunch Joe said, "We should talk to Hamilton's widow, Anne-Michelle Charbonneau. Wild child, party girl, philanthropist. She inherited a fortune from her father. Wedding or funeral, she always wears a black business suit, pearl earrings, and a pearl necklace, like she has just that one outfit. Divorced five times before she married Hamilton. She was in the process of divorcing him. Lives on El Camino Del Mar in Seacliff, the high end of the high end. Let's go over there. You're driving."

"Nice house," Joe said. "*Big* house."
"Italianate."
"What?"
"The architectural style."
"Aha."
Two Japanese gardeners tended the shrubbery.
Joe said, "Think we should use the tradesman's entrance?"
A Filipino maid answered the front door, Ben and Joe showed their badges, and the door closed. The lock clicked.
Joe said, "Is it cold out here or is it her?"
The door opened.
"She will see you. This way, quietly."
Polished marble floor. Walnut paneling. Hallway and closed doors. Two steps down to the living room. Thick carpet. Books

on coffee tables. Vaulted, beamed ceiling. Panoramic windows and views of the North American Strait, the Marin Headlands, and the Golden Gate Bridge.

The maid said, "Wait here."

Ben said, "Wow."

Behind him, Anne-Michelle Charbonneau laughed.

"Everyone says that when there's no fog. The view is an old friend of mine. I grew up in this house and when I was young I wondered where the freighters and passenger liners in the strait had been and where they were going. These days, I think about my life that way. Please sit down. I apologize for Maria. She is very protective of me."

Ben said, "I'm sorry for your loss."

"It's not quite the loss it would be under different circumstances."

Joe said, "Can you tell us, please, about your husband?"

"Mr. Last Word."

"Excuse me?"

"Ian always had to have the last word. He needed to be the smartest person in the room. The man had no peripheral vision."

"Ma'am?"

"He never looked to either side. There was Ian and what he wanted. And there was everything else."

"Why did you keep your name when you married him?"

"I gave it away five times. That was enough."

"Can you tell us why you and Mr. Hamilton separated?"

"He wouldn't stop sleeping around. You'd think a man on his third marriage would know better. He could have put up billboards: *Ian Christian Hamilton. At stud.* When I learned he was involved with his secretary, I confronted him. He said everyone knew about it and that—I am quoting him—I was the dumbest bitch he'd ever screwed. Then he got in his Porsche and left. He moved back to his penthouse."

"Your divorce . . ."

"I simply asked for my life back. He made it all very difficult, though no money or property were involved. I certainly didn't need his money. We maintained separate wills. My attorney can send you copies. I am not named as an heir in Ian's will and he is not named as an heir in mine. Yes, very difficult. He would be on the phone several times a day demanding one thing or another, then he wouldn't return my calls for a week. He had the nerve to claim mental cruelty and emotional duress."

"Did that make you angry?"

"Weary. Ian loved to grind people down. It seemed to give him strength."

"Can you think of anyone who would want to kill him?"

"Seriously? I'd say there's a long list."

Outside, Joe said, "Black business suit and pearl earrings. What did I tell you?"

Ben said, "I wanted to ask her, 'You knew his history. Why did you marry him? What did you expect?'"

"Maybe she thought her sixth time would be the charm. I don't know why people have to complicate their lives. What's up for tomorrow?"

"Mill Valley and the second Mrs. Hamilton, Laura Hayden. Painter, wood carver, well-known in Bay Area art circles. I hear she's a real firecracker. I'll drive."

Ben found the Hayden address and parked across the street.

"She's doing well. Perfect white stucco, painted tiles, iron gate, terra cotta roof, second-story balconies. All the authentic details of a Spanish Colonial Revival manse."

Red plaster hot lips ran the vertical length of the front door.

Joe said, "Probably not authentic."

"Ring my bell," said the lips. "Press my intercom button. Obey my commands. Ring. Press. Obey."

Joe laughed and said, "Better do what the lady says, Ben."

"Whoever you are," said the lips, "come through the side gate. The *side* gate! I'm in the studio. It's the only studio in my backyard. You can't miss it."

Laura Hayden stepped from behind an easel. Tall, slim, striking, barefoot. Short, spiked auburn hair. Paint-spattered jeans. Comfortably loose black t-shirt lettered in neon green script: *The jerk is dead.*

"Your names, gentlemen."

"Inspector Joe D'Alessandro and Sheriff's Deputy Ben Hyatt."

"Ah, yes. Ian. Dear, departed Ian. Hey, I didn't do it. Really, truly, I didn't."

She nodded toward a ship's figurehead, a likeness of Ian Hamilton. "Took me the whole second year of our marriage to carve that. We were going to buy a schooner and sail around the world."

"Joe said, "About Mr. Hamilton."

"Ian. No one ever called him Mister."

"Ian. How did you meet?"

"He came into my gallery. Said he liked my approach to color. Bought two expensive pieces. Commissioned a portrait. We got hot and steamy, it lasted longer than it usually does, and we woke up one morning in Paris, hungover and married."

"Did you have children?"

"Neither of us wanted the damn things. Anyway, Ian started cheating on me. He got into cocaine and group gropes a lot further than I was willing to go. He developed a fondness for hand-cuffs and mock rape—you know, where the woman is supposed to like it. And there was his fetish for pearl earrings, don't ask me to explain."

"Did Ian ever hurt you physically?"

"If he had I'd have been the one who shot him."

"His running around. Is that why you left?"

"Well, of course I was sick of his affairs, but when he said *I* should swing I refused. *He* told *me* to get out."

"Just like that?"

"Exactly like that. Ian's way or the highway. Selfish bastard was swinging and snorting with Anne-Michelle Charbonneau's crowd. He ended up buying me this house, my price for an easy divorce. For the record, I'm not sad or surprised that he's gone or that he went the way he did."

"Anything you'd care to add?"

"Ian was never wrong. Ian liked to win, to bruise, to dominate. He liked to cut people with words. That's what jerks do, isn't it? I once asked him where he got the idea he could do whatever he wanted. He said, 'Where do you get the idea I can't?' I think you'll find that he didn't have one single friend. Even dogs didn't like him."

"Naturally, we'd like to find whoever killed Ian. Is there anyone we should talk to?"

"I wouldn't know where to start. Ian left quite a trail."

"Ms. Hayden," Ben said, "did Ian ever mention someone named Edward Hayes?"

"Nice name. No."

In the car Joe said, "Your thoughts?"

"I'd rule out the firecracker."

"Agreed."

"Ditto Anne-Michelle Charbonneau."

"Even though she was deeply hurt?"

"Even though she was deeply hurt and could afford a world-class hit."

"Strange that Hamilton never had kids . . . except the one on the way."

"Thought they'd slow him down, I guess."

"Guys like him often reproduce themselves, if only by accident. Could be a ticked-off, disinherited son or daughter out there . . ."

"Ms. Hayden said he did coke."

". . . or an unpaid dealer. Maybe Hayes had the same supplier and the same problem."

"Let's go over to Hamilton's penthouse."

"Good thinking."

"One thing always leads to another."

"Morning interviews always lead to lunch. Let's find a good Italian deli, then go over to Hamilton's penthouse."

The Hamilton Apartments, five floors up, in the penthouse. Antique furniture and Persian carpets.

Ben said, "Familiar décor."

"He liked what he liked."

Well-stocked bar in the living room. Rolled $100 bills and white lines on a square glass plate. A portrait over the fireplace, signed by Laura Hayden, Hamilton done in neon green, purple, and orange. On the walls, photos of sailboats, sailing ships, and Ian Hamilton in Africa.

"Here's the foursome on the porch again," Ben said. "There's a Polaroid taped to the back of it. Same woman."

Long hair, long legs, short skirt, thin t-shirt, a smile that was equal parts innocence and invitation.

"A real beauty."

"What's in the bedroom?"

"The usual. Four-poster bed, handcuffs on each post, lubricants, pearl earrings, locked gun safe."

"Here, Joe. A shoebox full of Polaroids. Nothing but naked women. Various poses. First name and a date on each picture, all different, two or three a week for . . . three years. No phone numbers, so he probably didn't plan on seeing any of them more than once. Wait. There's a guy. Charles."

"Naked?"

"And ready for action. Another picture of Charles. And another. No dates."

A second bedroom served as a gym and home office. Treadmill, weights, tennis trophies and tennis racquets. Photos of Ian Hamilton courtside and dockside. An antique writing desk, a note in the only drawer: *You're wrong, Ian. It was never love. Sorry if you thought it was. Please stop calling. Don't come by. Don't write to me again. Charles.*

"What's next, Ben?"

"I want you to see where Hayes lived."

———————————

Ben said, "This is where we found Hayes, the guitar, and the newspaper on his desk. I'm pretty sure he was reading about Hamilton."

"Interesting."

"Let me show you around. You'll see that things are neat and tidy."

"Everything's first class. I'll bet the stereo cost more than my house."

"Tiffany lamps and Persian carpets. Where have we seen that before?"

"Gold records."

"And a platinum. That's big money. Hayes could have built a mansion. Instead, he put up a one-bedroom cottage. There are no pictures of people, no Rolodex. Just abstract art and two photos of his dog."

"Friends? Family?"

"None that we know of. If there's a will, we haven't found it."

"This place gives me the creeps, Ben. Too neat. Too tidy. Something's not right."

"I listened to his songs last night. The lyrics don't sound like him."

"How so?"

"They're about relationships with women. There isn't even a copy of *Playboy* around here."

"That might be the tip of an iceberg. Aha! Videotapes. Young boys. From someone named Jacques."

"I think it's time you met Mr. Hayes in person."

At the county morgue, a medical examiner pulled a sheet off Edward Hayes' body and began reading the autopsy report. "White male. Age about forty years. Five feet, five inches, 117 pounds. No evidence of disease or drugs." He put the report down.

"Okay, here's what you guys want to know. Two entry wounds, one exit wound. The head shot entered Hayes' left eye, passed through the frontal and temporal lobes, then down through the cerebellum, clipped the parietal bone, shattered the occipital bone—blew it off, I'd say—and exited the base of the skull. I found the expected fragments of copper and lead along the wound path. Most of the trauma is on the left side of the head. Classic JHP expansion. The bullet lodged in sheetrock behind Hayes. The other slug grazed the sternum before it penetrated the left ventricle and tore up his heart, broke a rib, and deflected downward. We found most of it in a kidney. There's a lot of internal tissue damage. Jacketed hollow points are supposed to stir things up. They do.

"Hayes was standing up for the first shot and lying on his back, crumpled against the wall, when he took the second. The first bullet—the one in the head—killed him. I'd call the one through the heart unnecessary. The shooter fired from seven, maybe eight, feet away. There's no powder residue on Hayes or his clothes, but there are traces on the books and newspapers that were on the desk. Both rounds are 9mm Luger. No one's claimed the body."

"I'm going back to Hayes' place tomorrow," Ben said. "I want to spend a day or two with his journals. He and Hamilton were looking for a roommate. I'll try to find out who that was."

4

January 1, 1966
17 years old today. I will assemble my life carefully and move forward.
Who shall I be?

January 28, 1966
Do not understand why I don't have any friends.

January 29, 1966
Father said he'd buy me a new car and support me through college. I
can leave home when I choose and go to any school I like if they'll
have me.

February 14, 1966
No longer a virgin! It happened in my room with Ronald! We kissed,
tore off our clothes, and did each other! I was so turned on! I can still
feel it! Want to try everything with him! Can't think of anything else.

February 18, 1966
A note, taped to the page.
Dear Edward —
My parents will be gone this weekend. Come over. I want you.
Ronald

August 23, 1967
Drove up to Sonoma County for college. Rural setting. Idyllic, small campus, only 1,400 students. Will start out living in a dorm to meet people and make some friends. Then I hope to find a house in the country.

September 6, 1967
No privacy at dorm.

September 9, 1967
My roommate requested a room change. He called me a fag. I paid extra to have the room to myself. I miss Ronald.

December 25, 1967
Home for Christmas. Ronald away somewhere. Lonely me.

January 1, 1968
Birthday party for one.

January 17, 1968
Fall semester is over. Straight A's without even trying. Father impressed. Lots of time to read, think, and play my guitar. No friends. Can't connect with anyone.

February 5, 1968
New semester, new roommate. Stephen. Is he?

February 9, 1968
Stephen is! We did it!

February 13, 1968
Stephen dropped out.

April 12, 1968
Saw Ronald over Spring Break. I'm saddle sore and happy. He still cares.

June 7, 1968
End of freshman year. Straight A's again. Three more years until my Bachelor's. No friends yet. Why is friendship so easy for everyone else?

August 2, 1968
Summer. Tutoring remedial English. Giving guitar lessons. Have ten paying customers, two are very pretty young boys. I like teaching. Might be a school teacher. Still don't have any friends. Too much free time. Maybe Ronald will visit.

September 9, 1968
Sophomore year. Paid extra again to have the room to myself.

October 6, 1968
Played and sang at Lefty's Bar & Grill open mic. Lots of applause for me! Then took three solos at the after-hours blues jam. More applause! People will notice me now.

October 13, 1968
One-night stand.

October 18, 1968
Open mic and blues jam. Another one-night stand.

November 8, 1968
Open mic. One-night stand. Want more than just one night!

November 15, 1968
Open mic. Applause!

December 8, 1968
What do I have to do? Still have no friends.

December 20, 1968
Open mic and blues jam. Threesome (my first! want more!) at nice house in Sonoma. It has a vineyard!

Christmas, 1968
Alone. The usual Christmas-birthday money from father. No word from Ronald.

December 31, 1968
New Year's jam and party at Lefty's. Went back to my room by myself.

January 1, 1969
Sad and alone on my 20th birthday. Ronald didn't even send a card.

February 10, 1969
Start of Spring semester. No dorm roommate, it's just easier.

April 24, 1969
Ian Hamilton. Classmate. Handsome. Possibly a friend or more?

June 5, 1969
End of semester. Still no friends.

August 1, 1969

Have become a regular at Lefty's open mic and blues jams. Playing a lot. No friends yet, maybe soon.

August 11, 1969

Amazing development! Ran into Ian Hamilton. He said, "Mr. Hayes, you and I were the only intelligent people in the class." He's rented a three bedroom Victorian and is looking for two housemates. Asked if I was interested. I went, but the house is completely empty. I said I didn't have any furniture. Ian's words: "Problem solved. My father owns a warehouse in San Francisco. We can pick out furniture for the house and our rooms. My father's men will deliver everything and set it up." Music to my ears!

August 25, 1969

Moved into the house with Ian Hamilton. Not in the country but have my own spacious room, it's gorgeous! Two Tiffany lamps. Antique desk and chair. Dresser. Persian carpet. Ronald will like my sleigh bed. Address is 805 Grove Street, Santa Rosa. Next week we start interviews for a roommate.

August 29, 1969

Ian. Is he or isn't he? He has a girlfriend, but maybe someday . . .

October 18, 1969

Ian gone every weekend, so have the house to myself. Not what I expected. It's a bit lonely. Still playing at Lefty's. Wish Ronald was here. Haven't heard from him.

November 3, 1969

New housemate, Tom Moyes. Handsome and wild. Dangerous? But Ian seems to like him and loaned him furniture. We all went down to the warehouse. Feel like I have two friends.

November 6, 1969
Tom in my bed. Good!

November 10, 1969
Tom.

November 11, 1969
Tom.

November 13, 1969
Tom.

November 14, 1969
Tom going away for two weeks.

December 2, 1969
Tom and Tom again.

December 8, 1969
Tom threatened to tell my father about us.

December 11, 1969
Tom says he did Ian and Ian did him.

December 12, 1969
Tom said he'll tell our parents if Ian and I don't come up with $1,000
each. I said I didn't have it.

December 17, 1969
Tom demanded money again. Ian hit him and he's gone. Don't think
he wrote to father.

Christmas, 1969
Comfort and joy with Ronald. Didn't tell him about Tom.

January 1, 1970
21st birthday. I can go to bars! Will play less at Lefty's and go to the city every weekend. Father likes my GPA and sent a very generous gift. I can live comfortably on it for an entire year! New housemate, John Barrow.

January 5, 1970
John isn't.

January 21, 1970
Private detective came to the house looking for Tom! Ian says don't panic.

January 22, 1970
Argued with Ian. He says we have to stay together until we know we're in the clear.

January 23, 1970
Huge argument with Ian.

January 26, 1970
John moved out. I came home and he'd left. Don't know why.

March 1, 1970
New housemate, Chris Reid. What a hunk!

March 4, 1970
Chris said no and made it clear I shouldn't have asked.

March 9, 1970
Huge argument with Ian about Tom.

March 12, 1970
Fight with Ian.

March 16, 1970
Fight with Ian.

March 23, 1970
Got beat up a little last weekend. Mr. Top played rough.

March 30, 1970
Fight with Ian.

April 2, 1970
Fight with Ian.

April 3, 1970
Truce.

April 5, 1970
Where is Ronald? Am I forgotten?

April 16, 1970
Chris moved out. Said he found a better place.

5

"Moyes. Barrow. Reid," Ben said. "Let's see if any of them turn up."

"I'm off to the coffee pot," Joe said. "Whoever's on the phone, I'll be back in a few minutes."

"They asked for you, said it's important."

"D'Alessandro...You lived in a house with Ian Hamilton? And a fellow named Edward Hayes. What is your name, sir? ...When can we talk to you, Mr. Barrow?"

Ben said, "Where to?"

"Lowell High School. Barrow's the principal. He said we'd find him in his office."

"Mr. Barrow," Joe said, "you know that Ian Hamilton is dead. Edward Hayes also died a few days ago."

"Hayes...What is going on?"

"We're trying to figure it out. What can you tell us about your old roommates?"

"They were smart, you couldn't take that away from them. But they wanted to control when I listened to music, when my friends could visit, how long a girlfriend could stay. Hamilton often called for lights-out at eleven. At times he acted like he owned the house and everyone in it. We shared chores, but three guys, you know, not much cleaning got done, except Hayes vacuumed and dusted the living room every day."

"Describe 805 Grove Street."

"Single-story Victorian, beautifully furnished. Three bedrooms, two bathrooms with clawfoot bathtubs, living room, formal dining room, eat-in kitchen, front porch. Attic, but Ian said no one ever went up there. I never did. I'll sketch the floor plan for you. Hamilton's room—quite elaborate, off the living room. Dining room here. Hayes' room here—white-painted walls and ceiling, gloss-black floor, oriental carpets, antique desk and chair, antique dresser, antique bed, antique lamps. Bathrooms here and here. Hayes and I shared this one. This was Hamilton's. My room, next to the kitchen area. New paint and a bare floor when I first saw it, but Hamilton took me to his father's warehouse and told me to choose whatever I wanted—carpet, bed, dresser, desk, chairs, lamps. I saw one carpet I liked. Well, I saw part of it. It was folded—all the others were rolled up—and I lifted a corner. Hamilton said it was stained and insisted I take another one, then he chose everything else to match. The next day, two men brought the furniture. It was all perfect and luxurious. I felt I was in his debt."

"You were all students?"

"Correct. Hamilton majored in philosophy. Hayes and I were on track for our teaching credentials."

"Did they quarrel?"

"Did they! Sometimes they argued in Hamilton's room. The door was always shut tight. Sometimes they sat in his car with the windows rolled up and yelled at each other. One time, they drove off and when they got back they weren't on speaking terms."

"Any idea what they argued about?"

"No, but I got the feeling that it was the same thing over and over again."

"Was there ever a sexual overture from either of them?"

"From Hayes."

"And?"

"I turned him down."

"How did he take that?"

"Like he was used to it."

"You lived there when?"

"For twenty-six days in January 1970."

"Not long. What happened?"

"Three weeks after I moved in, a private investigator came looking for someone named Thomas Alvin Moyes, whose last known address, he said, was 805 Grove Street. Moyes had disappeared. Foul play was suspected. Hamilton and Hayes told him they'd never heard of Moyes. A few days later I found two empty envelopes in my closet addressed to a Thomas Alvin Moyes at 805 Grove Street, official mail from the New Jersey State Attorney General. Six-week-old postmarks. I got out. Didn't spend another night there."

"Scared?"

"Terrified. Why did they lie? For all I knew, they'd killed Moyes and dumped his body somewhere."

"You didn't go to the police?"

"I had fear and a suspicion, nothing more. I calmed down."

"And you haven't been in contact with Hamilton or Hayes since you left?"

"No. I'd forgotten all about them until I saw Hamilton's picture on the evening news. Then I tried to collect my thoughts before I called you."

"Can you think of anyone who would harm Hamilton or Hayes or Hamilton *and* Hayes?"

"No. I hardly knew them."

Over coffee, Joe said, "Your thoughts, Ben?"

"Hayes mentioned Tom Moyes in his journal."

6

805 Grove Street, December 16, 1969, 11 p.m.

Raised voices in the living room, Edward Hayes and Tom Moyes.

"I told you, Tom! I don't have that much money!"

"Get it."

"Or you'll tell my father?"

"That's right. You're going to pay me $1,000 to keep quiet. So is Ian."

In his room, Ian Hamilton unplugged a desk lamp. He unscrewed the antique lampshade, laid it carefully on a chair, walked into the living room, and swung the lamp hard at the back of Tom Moyes' head. "There. He'll keep quiet and it won't cost us a dime."

"Ian! What did you just do?"

"Quick! Help me roll him in the carpet."

"What?"

"The carpet! Help me roll him up. He's getting blood on our floor."

"What have you done, Ian?"

"Shut up. I need to think. Okay, back your car into the driveway. Don't turn on the headlights. Open the trunk, then come in. We'll take him down the rear stairs. Move!"

On the stairs Edward said, "Why are we using my car?"

"We can't get blood in his."

"Oh."

"Don't worry. I wrapped his head. It won't leak. I'll drive his car, you follow in yours."

"Why?"

"Just follow me, Edward. There, he's in. Wait here."

Hamilton ran into the house. He was back in minutes carrying gloves, a shotgun and a box of shells, and a flashlight. After driving for an hour on country roads, he slowed then stopped at a locked gate.

"Headlights off, Edward."

"Where are we?"

"An apple orchard. That's all you need to know. Come hold the flashlight while I open up. Alright, let's roll Moyes out and lay him on his back under that tree. Good. Help me carry the carpet to your car. Good. Get in. Stay put. Don't touch his car."

Edward barely heard the shot.

Ian walked out of the orchard, locked the gate, and folded his gloves. "All done. Drive home."

"Where's the gun?"

"With Tom."

"But it's yours."

"Nobody knows that. It's old. Can't be traced. Besides, his fingerprints are all over it."

"Oh. His car?"

"It looks like he drove out here alone, doesn't it?"

"Tom said that you and he . . ."

"He lied."

"You killed him!"

"And you helped get rid of his body, which means you're in as deep as I am. Did you want him to tell your father? Well? Why so quiet all of a sudden, Edward? Answer me. Did you?"

"No! Of course not."

"Was there any other way? Anything else we could have done?"

"No."

"You can't talk to people like Tom, you can't reason with them. You have to fight them. They get what they deserve. Tom got what he deserved, didn't he? Well? Didn't he?"

"Yes, I guess so."

"He told my father."

"He told! But he promised he wouldn't if you paid him!"

"Tom thought I was a chump. He thought you were a chump. He would have kept coming back for more money, saying he'd tell other people if we didn't pay. It would've never stopped."

"What did your father say?"

"He said I should take care of it or he would. Now listen. If anyone asks, we've never heard of Tom Moyes. Stick to that, understand? Don't come apart on me and we'll be safe. His pockets are empty. I've got his wallet, and no one will ever know who he was. I'll take his things and the mucky carpet to the warehouse tonight. You scrub the living room floor while I'm gone. We should repaint it. My father's men will bring another rug and take away the furniture Moyes borrowed. Then we'll repaint his room. I'll place an ad for a new roommate. Okay, let's get Tom's clothes packed up and clear his stuff out of the bathroom. Don't keep anything that proves he was at the house. Tom wasn't smart. He wasn't prepared. He should have known that there's always something you don't expect. Things can happen quickly."

"I'm tired, Ian. I'm worn out."

"Let's get to work."

December 18, 1969
Ian wouldn't admit to me that he and Tom did it. But I know! I have Tom's notebook.

January 10, 1970
A crumpled sheet of paper in an envelope.
Edward —

Through a letter from one of your roommates and my own investigation, I have confirmed that you are a practicing homosexual. You are a disgrace to the family. Expect no further contact or money from me. You are disinherited. Sadly, your father

January 11, 1970
Keeping the car. Won't miss the old man. New semester coming up.

7

"Another Hamilton and Hayes roommate just called," Joe said. "Captain Chris Reid of the San Mateo Fire Department wants to talk about Ian Hamilton. He'll be home all day."

"We're on a roll."

"I'd like to hear from Moyes."

"Thank you for calling, Captain. Deputy Hyatt will ask the questions. I'll just listen."

Ben said, "Your roommates were Ian Hamilton . . ."

"Right."

". . . and Edward Hayes, also recently deceased."

"Hayes too?"

"What do you remember about them?"

"They were a strange pair. Hamilton ran the show. Hayes was a closet queen. Hamilton's follower. They weren't friends, but something kept them together. They argued a lot, always in Hamilton's room with the door closed."

"Argued about what?"

"I don't know. But they'd stay mad at each other for days."

"How did you meet them?"

"I answered their classified ad, 'room for rent in nice house,' or something like that. Well, it was more than nice. Antique furniture and Persian carpets everywhere. Paintings, silverware, gold-rimmed dishes. There were tapestries hanging in the living and dining rooms.

"Hamilton had a four-poster bed and he made a point of letting you know that he poked his girlfriend—a high-school brat named Joanna—on silk sheets. You wouldn't have believed his bedroom. Fancy wallpaper, framed paintings, thick oriental carpet, leather couch, Victorian writing desk, Tiffany lamps, velvet drapes.

"Hamilton and Hayes drove to San Francisco every weekend. I think they just wanted someone to look after the house while they were gone. Hayes said he stayed with a friend. Hamilton went home to his parents Friday afternoons. He'd go to class in the morning, return to pick up his mail and laundry, and leave. Even when I was there he'd lock the front door. He came back Monday evening."

"They drove down together?"

"Sorry. Not together."

"Did Hamilton have any visitors?"

"Just the schoolgirl."

"You said Hamilton and Hayes were strange."

"Very. Hamilton always took his shoes off before he went into his room, and if you went in for an audience with his majesty you took yours off. Hayes washed other people's dishes because they didn't sparkle enough. He insisted that cleaning the living room was his job and his alone. A couple times he came back from San Francisco with bruises on his face. Said he fell down some stairs. Twice? The boy got into some rough trade. Who did he think he was fooling?

"Hamilton liked to tell people what to do. His furniture, his rules, you know? I was just back from Nam and didn't need that shit. After a couple of weeks I started looking for another place. One night my girlfriend and I were in my room and I heard a floorboard creak outside my door. Later, she heard the same thing when she was in the bathroom. It was Hayes, listening. Hamilton would come out of his room wearing boxer shorts, all sweaty from banging his princess, and get a glass of water at the kitchen sink. He'd grin, drain the glass, and then go back to his room. Probably didn't offer his beloved a drop. Come to think of it, Hayes never brought anyone home and no one ever came to see him. When my army buddies dropped by, he'd pin notes to his towels in the bathroom, 'Do not use! These are mine!'"

"Anything else?"

"Hayes was a snoop."

"Why do you say that?"

"I found him reading old letters I'd tossed in the trash. He said he was looking for something he'd thrown out. Books on my desk, underwear in the dresser—sometimes they weren't quite where I left them. I kept a .38 Special in my desk drawer, laid a certain way. It didn't move itself."

"Did Hamilton or Hayes ever come on to you?"

"Hayes did. I told him I liked women and he backed off."

"Nice house, but not nice roommates?"

"That's right. I bailed when I found a decent apartment. I'll tell you, though, I heard Hayes play his guitar a couple of times. He was phenomenal. He could sing, too. He was a different person with that guitar in his hands."

"When did you live there?"

"March and most of April 1970."

"You haven't seen Hamilton or Hayes since?"

"No reason to."

"Ideas on who might want them dead?"

"Haven't got a clue. They were harmless screwballs. They argued about the proper way to put a toilet paper roll on the holder. You don't hose guys for that."

8

Joe — I've gone to chat with a friend at the FBI office. Meet me at Jake's around noon? I'm buying. Ben.

"I've already ordered," Ben said. "Here's what I've got on Ian Hamilton. Attorney, solo practice specializing in divorce. Yachtsman. Tennis player. Ladies' man. Born San Francisco, 1949. Married Joanna Papadopoulos right after he graduated from college. He was twenty-two, she was barely eighteen. They toured Europe for a year, a wedding gift from his father. Then he went to law school in San Francisco for three years. Daddy paid for that too. Hamilton passed the California Bar Exam the first time. Five years into the marriage, reports of infidelity and spousal abuse surfaced. There were visits to emergency rooms, photos of bruises, and charges. Each time, Joanna withdrew her complaints. They separated. Six years after that and still legally married to him, she slit her wrists in a hotel bathtub. They didn't have any kids.

"He spent three years chasing skirts, settled a paternity suit out of court, and paid for two abortions. Married Laura Hayden. That lasted three years. Married Anne-Michelle Charbonneau. After two years she'd had enough. Hamilton died one year later."

Joe said, "Let me tell you about Hamilton Sr., known as Big Jim. He ran protection schemes, brothels, speakeasies. Made his bones at sixteen. Had a fleet of trucks, brought liquor in from

Canada during Prohibition, and told every judge who would take a bribe that he was in the household moving business. Big Jim never served a day in prison. Ten years ago—long after he'd quit the rackets—someone emptied a Thompson magazine into him. Twenty rounds. He was eating dinner at his favorite restaurant. Blood and parts of Big Jim were everywhere. They had to replace the carpet."

"Even ten years ago the Thompson was a little out of date."

"A message from the old days."

"Ever find out who or why?"

"No. I don't recall that anyone cared, so it went cold right away. But somebody knew. Somebody always knows."

"I got to thinking about what John Barrow told us. I searched the FBI's Missing Persons File for Thomas Alvin Moyes. He's linked to the New Jersey State Attorney General and a Sonoma County Coroner's Report dated September 1970. I called the New Jersey AG's office and they checked their records. Moyes was an informant with a blown cover, on the run from people who didn't want him to testify. The AG didn't want them to know that Moyes had died. Without him there was no case. So the coroner agreed to tell the press he couldn't ID Moyes' remains, which were in an orchard near Sebastopol.

"Here's the coroner's report, complete with photographs. A shotgun found with Moyes had the same engravings as the shotgun we saw in the Hamilton warehouse."

"The missing half of the matched pair."

"You know, the coroner actually thought Moyes committed suicide."

"Suicide, my butt. Look at the photos. He shot himself in the chest and the back of his skull was nothing but bone fragments? How could the coroner miss that?"

"The report says he fell backwards when he pulled the trigger and his head hit a rock."

"It would take more than a fall like that to turn his skull into bread crumbs."

"Empty lower barrel, one spent shell in the upper barrel, 12-gauge shells in Moyes' car, but no wallet. Would a suicide toss his own wallet?"

"Maybe."

"Or maybe Ian Hamilton did."

"I'd put money on that."

"Tracing the gun would have led to the Hamiltons."

"The coroner did them a favor."

"Big Jim owned the orchard. Ian Hamilton inherited the property. Never sold or developed it."

"Interesting."

"I'll go up there tomorrow. Probably won't be much to see, but I'm curious."

Even with a map Ben couldn't find the orchard. He stopped at a farmer's fruit stand to ask for directions.

"The old apple farm? Must be at least fifteen acres. It's all wild and grown over, but the land is worth a fortune. I heard they found a skeleton there once. Go out to Apple Tree Road. Take the second gravel driveway on the right. The first goes to a vacant house. When I came here twenty years ago a nice young couple lived in it. They split up. There's a locked gate, just climb over it like everyone else does."

———————

"I couldn't help it, Joe. The place felt more like a graveyard than an old orchard. Who knows how many friends and associates Big Jim buried out there? It's just weeds and dead apple trees now. And old tennis balls, lots of them, some chewed in half."

"Dogs do that. Somebody had a dog."

9

May 20, 1970
Starting to relax about Tom. I now think Ian is right. Say nothing and it will fade away.

May 23, 1970
Will I ever hear from Ronald again?

May 24, 1970
Dearest Edward —

How is my darling? I'm working at Finocchio's! I dress up like Katherine Hepburn, she is so divine. My stage name is Ronalda Hepburn. Like it? I do my act four nights a week. Not much money, but I sizzle and sing. Guys get so horny watching me they can't walk! They pay tons of money to get into bed with a pro. Come live with me for the summer. I've got the most wonderful-best apartment! Can't wait until you're in my arms. I miss you. Ronald/Ronalda

June 10, 1970
New housemate, and just in time. David Copeland. Very handsome. He'll watch our home over the summer while Ian and I are away. I leave tomorrow (three months in San Francisco with Ronald!), then Ian leaves for Europe. David plays guitar quite well. He's at least as

good as I am, maybe better. We jammed, good session! Ian said we're not really playing unless we have sheet music! Jealous boy!

Ian Hamilton stood in the doorway of Edward's bedroom. Edward, out of sight but not quite out of mind. Edward, nervous and weak but, hopefully, smart enough to keep quiet. When his father had asked if Edward should be taken care of, he'd said no, after Tom Moyes it would draw attention to the house, and the old soldier had replied, "You have become a man of good judgment. You can always reconsider." Ian walked outside, where David Copeland was lowering the hood of his Jeep.

Ian said, "I guess it's just us until I ship out. That's a beautiful armoire in your room. Antique?"

"Probably. It's been in my family for generations."

"I have an idea. Edward and I painted your room a subtle off-white and gave it a gloss-black floor, but it needs a few finishing touches. I know the perfect carpet for you. We should also get furniture to match your armoire. Your bedroom could be as palatial as Edward's. It won't cost you anything."

"No thanks. I've got what I need."

"Are you sure? I can promise you there's a lot of fine antique furniture at my father's warehouse in San Francisco."

"Thanks, Ian. I'm comfortable."

"Oh, come to the city with me. We can get to know each other on the way down. I'll give you a private, personal tour of Hamilton Storage. You've never seen anything like it. It's quite a show."

Ian's car blocked the sidewalk in front of the warehouse. He tapped the horn. "My father also owns the office building across the street. I don't know what I'll do with it when I inherit." A massive steel door slid open. Ian eased his car into a dark garage, he tapped the horn again, and the door closed. He turned off the engine. "Listen."

David said, "To what?"

"To nothing. When the door is shut you can't hear anything outside and out there you can't hear what goes on inside. My father used to say that the place is quiet as a casket. He had it built special. Any minute now . . ."

Rows of fluorescent ceiling lights sputtered. Electric motors hummed. Ventilation fans began to turn.

"Lights, camera, action. Those old trucks are from my father's moving company. The next floor up is European art and statues. The third floor is, hell, I don't know. It's all boxes and crates stacked to the ceiling. Carpets and furniture are on the fourth floor. If you see something you like up there, just say so. We can take the freight elevator."

Ian lifted the elevator gate at the fourth landing. "This is my floor. I love it. Lots of windows, sunlight, views of the city. I might make part of it into an office someday, or maybe I'll turn the whole floor into a bachelor pad and bring women up in the elevator. Well, take a look around."

One floor, one room. Brick walls and concrete columns. Antique tables. Tiffany lamps. Rolled up carpets. Leather chairs. An engraved shotgun in an open gun case.

"Half of a matched pair," Ian said. "No idea where the other one went."

"Nice gun."

"Anything catch your eye?"

"No. Really, I'm set."

"You're really sure, absolutely sure."

"Positive. Thanks anyway."

"Well, if I can't convince you that my furniture is classier than yours, at least take a carpet to cover your bare floor. I know just the one. I'll tell my father's men to bring it to the house."

Ian looked down at the busy street. "Lee Harvey Oswald could have had a field day from up here."

Now that Ian was finally gone, David thought, he'd have the house to himself for three months, something he'd been looking forward to. He unrolled a poster on the dining room table.

The Brass Rail presents David Copeland
Accompanying himself on guitar
Original folk, blues, and contemporary
Friday and Saturday, June 19 and 20
Two sets each night

Friday night.

The Brass Rail. Happy Hour. Full house. Girls' night out.

"God, Kate, you were right. David Copeland is *very very very* good looking. I'm gonna eat him up!"

"I saw him first."

Saturday night.

In the audience, moving to the beat, her eyes on his. Prettiest girl in the crowd. Then she was sitting next to him at the bar.

"I think we're neighbors," she said. "You live at 805 Grove and drive an old Jeep."

"And you live down the block in the brick house."

"Kate Anderson."

"Excuse me, Kate. I'd like to stay and talk, but my second set is coming up."

Sunday night.

House lights on, old Jeep in the driveway. She climbed the stairs and rang the bell.

"Kate. Hi."

"I know it's late. I hope I'm not interrupting anything."

"It's okay. Come in."

"Are you busy?"

"I'm writing a song. *Trying* to write a song."

"Your songs are good. Everybody says so. *I* say so."

"Thanks, but it's just something I do in my spare time."

"Would you like to . . ."

"I've been thinking . . ."

". . . kiss me?"

". . . I've been thinking that I'd like to."

"Do it. Let's see what happens."

Monday morning.

It took Kate a minute to remember where she'd spent the night. David.

Where was he?

In daylight, she saw that his room was unlike other men's bedrooms she'd known. It could have been an artist's den, almost filled by a double bed, desk, armoire, and leather easy chair. A wooden airplane propeller took up one corner, an old guitar case another. An oriental carpet—what she could see of it—covered the floor. Clamps on the desk and headboard supported swing-arm lamps.

At the foot of the bed a wooden shipping crate served as a catch-all table for seashells, fossils, arrowheads, guitar picks and strings, a Nikon camera and lenses, yellow boxes of photographic slides, spare change, snapshots of David: legs dangling from a truck tailgate; wearing a backpack on a mountain trail; holding a rattlesnake by the tail.

Books were piled on the floor and jammed between brick-and-board shelves. Plato, Shakespeare, Conrad, London, Hemingway, biology, geology, architecture, music theory, Steinbeck, art history. Asimov, Thoreau, Salinger. Photography, Kesey, Heller, Twain, Vonnegut, Kerouac. Field guides for birds, trees, rocks, mammals, and reptiles. A Jeep repair manual.

Record albums leaned against a pair of loudspeakers. On the desk, headphones, a turntable, and an amplifier crowded stacks of notebooks and an ancient typewriter.

Unframed art prints and poster-sized photographs had been push-pinned to every wall. *Nighthawks. Girl with a Pearl Earring. The Starry Night.* Yosemite. Grand Canyon. Jackson Hole. Fallingwater.

Inside a doorless closet, neat rows of jeans, t-shirts, and folded work shirts lined a wall of shelves. A backpack, sleeping bag, and binoculars hung from wooden pegs above hiking boots, moccasins, cowboy boots, and snowshoes.

Atop the armoire, a gallon jar held a snake skeleton coiled around two plastic mice; the posed bones of a bird, wings spread wide, perched on a flat rock; an animal's skull gripped an identification tag—*Vulpes macrotis*—in its teeth. Tarnished picture frames held black-and-white photographs: a soldier in a war-ravaged city, grinning, holding a short rifle and a helmet torn through by one jagged hole. The same man, tuxedoed, seated at a piano. A young woman. The man and the woman together, her hand on his, cutting a tall wedding cake.

An aroma of strong coffee drifted into the room. She lay back. Last night ... so *that* was what everyone talked about. She'd never, not like that. But men didn't care. In, out, good night, goodbye, and David Copeland would probably tell her that he had things to do, that she should just leave.

Kate dressed slowly, still amazed, still looking around the room. She straightened the sheets, fluffed David's pillows, and took a deep breath. Ready for another brush-off, she opened the bedroom door.

At the kitchen table, David closed the book he was reading and smiled. "Hi. I didn't want to wake you. I get up early. Coffee? A shower? A soak in the tub? There's clean towels. I'll have breakfast ready when you come out. Look, ah, last night was incredible and, ah, I'd like to do it again, that is if you . . ." He laughed. "What have we done?"

In the tub, she realized that she hadn't said a word. Over breakfast he said, "I want to go to the coast today and walk on a beach with you. Stay with me tonight?"

The next morning Kate said, "I've got to go home."

"Come back soon. Here's a key."

That evening, she let herself in.

"Ah, Kate. You take my breath way."

"I've had you on mind all day. Kiss me. Feel my heartbeat. Take off your clothes."

Nights in David's bed became weeks spent together. Time and again Kate looked around his room, an open book on his life, a new chapter in hers. Manilla envelopes bulged with notes, sketches, and photographs from David's road trips. Big Sur. Canyonlands. Joshua Tree. Yellowstone. Jasper and Banff. Memphis, Nashville, New Orleans. She thought his pen-and-ink drawings of owls, eagles, and herons belonged in a museum. His record albums and old 78s, more than she'd ever seen in one person's collection, contained music she'd never heard of. How did he ever find it? He said he'd taken a year off from school. What did he do, see, learn?

Every day brought new questions. She pointed to his bird skeleton.

"What is that?"

"Raven. Mr. Nevermore."

"Ha. And these bones?"

"Rattlesnake. Mr. R."

"What's with the propeller?"

"Found it in Saline Valley, the perfect place."

"And the skull. *Vulpes macrotis*? Is that how you pronounce it?"

"Yes. Kit fox, also from Saline Valley. We should go someday."

"Where is it?"

"Not far from Death Valley. You drive down a long unpaved road to get there. It's a desert. Mountains all around. I know a campsite near a waterfall and a place to swim, and there are natural hot springs a few miles away."

"You backpack alone. Why?"

"Solitude."

"Do you get scared or lonely?"

"Never."

"What about the real world? People. Electric lights."

"For me, the natural world is just as real. Sometimes it's all I need. Kate, why don't you move in? You practically live here now. You hardly ever go home."

"I don't go home because I don't want to let you out of my sight. My God! I've never felt like this."

"We can squeeze my things into the closet. The armoire's all yours. It belonged to my mother."

"Hey."

"Hey what?"

"My girlfriends say I've got an old man."

"What do you tell them?"

"I tell them, 'Yeah, I do. He's kind and sweet and great in bed. He's a mellow dude.'"

David would pick up his guitar, sing a few words, write and rewrite a line, then rewrite it again. Kate loved listening to him. Loved the way his fingers moved on the fretboard. The way his forearm muscles rippled when he played. The way his hands felt on her skin.

10

August 21, 1970
Argued with Ronald and came home a few days early. He can be such a bitch sometimes! David Copeland has a girlfriend living here. Not sure how I feel about that because David is such a fine guitar player. He writes great songs! He gets paying gigs! We've jammed several times and will work up a few numbers and do open mic at Lefty's. Ian's not coming back for a couple weeks. We'll see what he says about Kate Anderson.

August 23, 1970
My Dear Edward —
Why so angry? You know what I do for a living. My clients pay me then I pay rent and buy food. $500 for a threesome? Hello, you bet! Sex for money doesn't mean a thing, so please don't be jealous. You and I can still be who we are to each other. Ronald

August 30, 1970
I did open mic at Lefty's with David last night. Fantastic! For our encore we played one of David's songs, "Nothing Personal." The audience went crazy so we did another, "Listen To Me," brought the house down, and did another, "I'll Let You Know." I've found a music partner and a friend! We should make a demo tape!

September 3, 1970
I am afraid.

The Press Democrat, September 2, 1970
Grisly Find in Abandoned Sebastopol Orchard
A human skeleton was discovered in an orchard west of Sebastopol yesterday, according to Sonoma County Coroner Jay Osman. A gun and an automobile were recovered at the scene. "The remains are badly decomposed and identification may be impossible," Osman said. "The car was reported as stolen last year. That's all I can say at this time."

September 6, 1970
Ian came back late last night. Showed him the newspaper article. He said he'd forgotten about Tom and not to worry because there's nothing that links us to him. Told Ian about the girl. He's not happy about it and will talk to David. He wants me to be there.

"Good morning, Ian," David said. "How was Europe?"

"Incredible women, incredible wine, incredible food, in that order. Now look. About your lady friend."

"Kate? What about her?"

"I don't want females living here. Occasional romantic visits are acceptable, but 805 isn't a party house. We agreed in June that we're here to study."

"Kate studies."

"Studies what?"

"English. She reads a lot. And she works."

"What work?"

"Part-time modeling for department stores."

"Oh, really."

"Yes, really. She found time to keep the house clean. You should thank her. And she planted flowers in the pots on the front porch. She thought you'd like that."

"Does she provide other services?"

"Stop right there."

"Sorry. When is she moving out?"

"She isn't."

"No women."

"Fine. We'll leave."

"Wait," Edward said. "We can work this out. Ian, why shouldn't they stay?"

"I didn't say they shouldn't stay."

"But that's what you meant. If David and Kate go, I go."

"Not so fast. Can I talk to you for a minute? In my room."

Closing his bedroom door, Ian said, "Don't forget, Edward, you and I have a tie that binds. We need to stick together until we know we're safe. So, okay, she stays, he stays, you stay. Well, where's the woman hiding? When do I get to meet this Kate?"

"Kate," David said. "Ian. Ian, Kate."

Ian said, "David, you didn't tell me your friend was so attractive." In their room, Kate said, "I didn't like the way Ian looked at me."

"He is a bit of a pig, isn't he?"

"I heard what he said about services. I'm not cleaning the house anymore. He can do it."

September 7, 1970

First Ian says that nothing connects us to Tom, then he says stick together. I think he's just keeping an eye on me. I need to stay here with David. He'll understand that I'm his friend and that we could make tons of money with his songs. Not sure how the girl will fit in Our music has to come first.

September 10, 1970
Listened last night. David and Kate laughed a lot and made love.

September 29, 1970
Safe!

The *Press Democrat*, September 28, 1970

Coroner Rules Suicide

A skeleton found in an orchard earlier this month appears to be that of a male in his mid-twenties. "We do not know who he was," said the coroner. "The evidence suggests that death resulted from a self-inflicted gunshot wound. At present, we do not have the resources to pursue the matter further."

October 7, 1970
Ian wants us all to sit for a group photo. He says there's a professional photographer who owes his father a favor and that everyone will get framed copies.

October 21, 1970
David and Kate went dancing. Looked through David's notebooks. He's written more songs than he's let on. Hoped to look in his wood crate but he keeps it locked and I couldn't find the key.

November 3, 1970
We are packing them in at Lefty's!

November 8, 1970
The word is out and we're getting real gigs every weekend! Not much money, but better than just applause. No more open mic! David doesn't understand that we're sitting on a gold mine. Kate seems a bit cold lately. Is she jealous? Will she try to take David away from me?

———————————

November 26, 1970
We're in Rolling Stone, Issue Number 71! Sent an autographed copy
to Ronald!

Who Are These Guys?

David Copeland and Edward Hayes have been thrilling audiences in Bay Area clubs in Oakland, Berkeley, and, lately, San Francisco, where we caught up with them between sets at The Matrix. The duo and their well-played acoustic guitars have gained a following. They go by a different made-up-on-the-spot name each weekend. Prurient Interest, Nervous Laughter, The Irritations, Wretched Excess, Patchy Hair Loss, and Two Thoughtless Bastards, to name a few. Copeland and Hayes sound, at times, like one person singing harmony with himself. Their seamlessly-traded rhythm and lead guitar parts are full of surprises. There's something going on here.

Tell me about David Copeland and Edward Hayes.

DC—We're college students. I'm in biology. Ed's going for a teaching credential. We play for fun. There's certainly no real money in it.

EH—Yet.

DC—And no one's throwing underwear at us.

EH—But we wouldn't complain.

How did you get together?

EH—David happened to move into the house where I live. He plays, I play. The rest is history.

Rumor has it Connection Records wants you to sign a record deal.

EH—It's not a rumor. They want us to move to Los Angeles.

David, your songs lean toward the dark side.

DC—Yeah. Imagine that, a cheerful guy like me.

Are they autobiographical?

DC—Sort of. It's hard to write what you don't know.

Your musical influences?

DC—Folk, jazz, blues, rock, R&B, country, Western swing, you name it. Turns out, Ed likes a lot of what I like. Lately, we've been into Delta blues, Robert Johnson in particular. Can't get enough RJ.

EH—Django Reinhardt, too.

Ah, Django.

DC—Pure genius.

Nice guitars. Martins?

DC—Oh, yeah. Ed's is a particularly mellow 1951 00-18. My D-28 dates from 1959. It's a cannon. People have offered to buy it. It's not for sale.

EH—I'd like to say that my guitar isn't for sale either and that we're thinking of adding a Telecaster to the mix.

People are talking about your songs. Tell me about "My Heart Is Frozen Solid."

DC—An early attempt at a three-chord country song. Couldn't sell it, wasn't surprised. Too many chords, I guess.

"Shaking The Devil's Hand."

DC—A friend went to heroin. He died on his 18th birthday.

"I'll Let You Know."

DC—A woman is about to leave her man. Or is she?

"Nothing Personal."

DC—Just like it says.

"Take It From Me."

DC—A portrait of an exceptionally self-centered ex-girlfriend. No names.

"Read The Fine Print."

DC—Relationships.

"Don't Let It Stop You."

DC—Sex.

"And Then?"

DC—What happens after we sleep together?

Good question. "Listen To Me."

DC—Or I'll walk out the door.

"Coffin Nail."

DC—That's it, we're done, I'm gone.

"Like a Hammer On My Heart."

DC—Broken heart, broken man.

"Clean Slate."

DC—Starting over.

You've written many more.

DC—Well, yes. Songwriting's a hobby, really. I jot down lyrics when they come to me. I always carry pencils and a notebook and I get back to the words when a melody suggests itself. Then I work things out on my guitar, usually late at night.

People say you're another James Taylor and that you and Edward could be the next Simon and Garfunkel.

Hayes smiles eagerly. Copeland frowns and says, "That's quite a compliment, but there's already a Taylor, a Simon, and a Garfunkel. We're not in their league. Not even close."

EH—David and I entertain a friendly disagreement about that.

DC—Well, I know Ed wants to make records, hire a band, and tour Europe, but I'm happy to stay in school and work the local music scene.

Have you been playing a long time?

EH—I started when I was nine.

DC—Got my first guitar for my fifth birthday. My father played piano and sax in dance bands and on jazz recordings, so I grew up around music. Again, it's only a hobby. I'm focused on my degree.

Maybe so. But Copeland and Hayes are good. Very good. The door is wide open for them and they can walk through if they want to. David Copeland's songs could take them a long way.

December 2, 1970

My money will be gone in a few months. Asked David to think seriously about signing with Connection Records.

December 9, 1970

Jacques, Connection Records rep, and I had a talk with David. We could all make a lot of money, but David is undecided. I sense that Kate is the reason. I don't think she likes me. I don't think I like her either.

December 10, 1970

I tried again to get David to see the money angle.

December 12, 1970

Heard David sing "Plenty of Time" to Kate. It's a beautiful song! His best. He never told me about it. Could make us a fortune.

December 19, 1970

Connection Record still wants us. David says he needs more time to think about a recording contract and the commitment, then he'll talk it over with Kate. Ugh.

December 24, 1970

Ronald invited me to his Christmas party. Why so late? Ian with family for the holidays. David and Kate went camping. A place called Saline Valley. I can't believe that's more important than our music. We skipped two paying gigs! I need money! Must talk to David as soon as he comes back.

"We've got a real future here, David. We'll have money, more than we ever dreamed of. A few years in the music business and we'd be set for life. I'll buy a house in the country and you'll buy whatever you like. Then we can go back to school."

"If you quit school, you'll lose your deferment. Do you think you'll be happy in the army? You'll have problems. I'm sorry, Ed. I'd like my doctorate sooner rather than later. I don't care about the money."

January 11, 1971
Jacques and I had another talk with David, who's still not ready to sign a contract. I called Jacques later. He says we can't record the songs without David's signature. Connection Records won't risk a lawsuit over the copyrights. If only the songs belonged to me!

February 15, 1971
Jacques stopped by the house and talked to David alone. Are they planning a move without me?

February 16, 1971
Argued with David. Money almost gone.

March 3, 1971
Surprise visit from Ronald. He was in drag and Kate saw him. I told him before, don't come to the house like that! He's posed for two magazines. Said it pays well and I should think about it since I need money and if I was really broke I'd sell my guitar. We got into an argument and he stormed out, so I drove down to his place. We made up and went straight to the bedroom. He loaned me $500. I really do love him.

March 4, 1971
Came back and fought with Kate. Damn her! She is against me!

March 18, 1971
David and Kate gone for a week. Connected with Ian! Two times last night in his room! He: very drunk, passionate, receptive. Me: very turned on.

March 22, 1971
Ian says it didn't happen.

March 27, 1971
Pleaded with David to change his mind. Will settle things with Ian tonight.

"You liked it, Ian!"

In their bed, Kate stirred and said, "David, it's Ian and Edward again."

"What? Another fight. It's 2 a.m. I'll tell them to keep it down."

In the dining room, Edward shouted, "You did it with Tom, you did it with me! You liked it! I should tell your father!"

Ian pressed the muzzles of his shotgun against Edward's chest. "You can't prove anything," he said. "That's the point, remember? That's how the game is played."

"Ian," David said. "Ian! Give me the gun."

Ian stood for a moment, silent, angry, glaring at Edward.

"Give me the goddamn gun, Ian."

"Here! Jesus! It's not even loaded!"

David took the shotgun, broke it open, and looked into the breech. Clean brass. Undented primers.

The door to Edward's room slammed shut.

David said, "What was all that, Ian?"

"I don't want to talk about it."

"Fine. I'll hold onto the gun until you cool off."

David walked back to the bedroom, closed the door, and pulled the shells from the cartridge chambers.

"You need to get away from them," Kate said. "We should have a place of our own."

"You're right. It's time."

"I'll find us something."

"I'm tired of their little war. No more gigs, no more Jacques, no more talk about money and houses in the country. I'll tell Ed in the morning. At least I got them to stop shouting."

But in the morning Edward was gone and Ian was shouting again. "That little rodent stole two of my Tiffany lamps!"

March 31, 1971

It's over between me and Ian. Hate to say goodbye to my room, but don't want to end up like Tom. Two months until graduation. Then what? Almost out of money again.

After searching for a week, Kate rented a small house and a barn on two acres west of Sebastopol.

"It's off Apple Tree Road," she said, "next to an old orchard where no one goes. I think you'll like it. The nearest neighbor is half a mile away. Let's move in this weekend."

"Let's plant a garden."

"Let's get a dog."

A candlelight dinner for two. A shared bottle of wine. Kate's chicken cacciatore.

She said, "I wish I could have seen Ian's face when he came back and our room was empty. Did you leave a note?"

"Just the keys, his carpet, and his shotgun. He'll figure it out."

"Goodbye, Ian."

"We're alone out here."

"It's perfect. Like Saline Valley."

"Marry me, Kate? I can't support a family yet, but . . ."

"I can wait."

One week later David sped up the driveway leaning hard on the Jeep's horn.

"You won't believe this, Kate. I hardly believe it myself. The biology department offered me a part-time teaching job. It's an honor and I want it. The pay will cover our rent, so that's good, but office hours, grading papers, and prepping for lectures will cut into our time together. Field trips are going to keep me away for three or maybe four days."

"I'll be okay because I'll know you're coming back."

It was sweet to teach the outdoor field classes, sweet to watch his students learn, sweet to be accepted as a colleague by his professors, sweet to come home to Kate at the front door, eager for their loving, saying, "Tell me about your trip later."

———————

Kate called her sister. "Carol, help me. I'm never late."

———————

David returned from his fourth field trip to empty wine bottles on the kitchen counter and Kate asking, "Are you screwing coeds?"

"Jesus. Where'd that come from? No, absolutely not. Some people want to teach and some want to learn."

Kate poured herself a glass of wine. "I miss you, okay? I need you. I want you all to myself."

"You're drinking more, you're smoking more weed, and you've stopped going to your classes."

"Weed makes music sound so good. Food tastes better. *You* taste better. When you're here."

"There's a one-week conference coming up in Yosemite. Why don't you come with me? We could go hiking or whatever you like. You'll meet some really nice folks."

"We'll see. What do you want for dinner?"

"Chicken cacciatore."

"Then you're going to the grocery store."

David walked the aisles, thinking that he and Kate should get to know a few people, invite them over, and build up some social contacts for her. They lived in their own world when he was home, but she was by herself most of the time, losing interest in everything, drinking and getting stoned, waiting for him. She should have a companion, maybe even the dog she wanted.

Pinned to a bulletin board outside the store he found a hand-lettered flyer: *Purebred Chocolate Lab. Female. Two years old. Spayed. Friendly. Likes tennis balls and car rides. Not too bright. $10.* He called the owner, drove over to meet the dog, and went home to Kate.

"Let's go for a ride," he said. "Got something to show you."

When she first saw the dog, Kate said, "Oh, David, she's beautiful. I'm in love."

"She's yours. What's her name?"

"She looks like a Molly."

The Lab ran to David, dropped a tennis ball at his feet, and licked his hand.

"Ooh," Kate said. "She likes you."

"Let's take Molly and her tennis ball home."

Walking in the orchard that afternoon, David said, "Molly, where's Kate?"

The dog looked at Kate.

"How could she know your name? Molly, find Kate."

Molly moved to Kate's side and sat down.

Kate said, "Good girl, Molly, my new friend."

"Molly," David said, "I think it was your owner who wasn't too bright."

————————

David phoned three times from the road and once from the campus. The Yosemite conference had been cancelled, he wanted to tell her. He loved her, he loved Molly, he'd be home tonight, three days early. Did she want to do anything special—go out to dinner or to a concert, or go car camping at the coast with Molly? They'd have an unbroken week together.

Kate didn't answer the calls and he began to worry. He knew how far away she was from help. Or maybe she'd gone for a long walk with Molly, who had taken to digging up the orchard.

David turned into their driveway. There were no lights, odd because Kate stayed up past midnight and always left the porch light on. He shut off the engine and listened. Just crickets. He pulled a tire iron from the Jeep's toolbox.

Dark house.

Quiet house.

Someone's pickup truck by the front stairs, driver's door open, keys in the ignition.

David gripped the tire iron, stepped through the front door and felt along a wall for a light switch.

"Kate?"

Molly whined and pressed against him.

The living room reeked of pot and cigarettes. An LP spun on the turntable, the needle stuck in a return groove. His Martin leaned against a table's edge, about to fall over. He laid the guitar in its case, took a flashlight from a kitchen drawer, said, "Find Kate," and followed Molly to the bedroom.

On the night stand: syringe, tourniquet, joints in a baggie, a hash pipe fashioned from aluminum foil.

On the bed: Kate and a man, spooned under a crumpled sheet. "Be cool," the man said, "be cool." He half-rolled, half-fell to the floor and curled into a fetal ball. Molly nosed Kate's arm, climbed up, and lay against her.

"Kate," David said, "What are you doing?"

She came back from wherever she was to whisper his name.

He pulled clothing from his closet. Cleared his desk. Placed the guitar case by the front door. Made two trips to the Jeep and filled the back seat. Took one last look around the living room. Carried his notebooks out of the house. Molly followed, hoping for a ride. He led her to the front stairs and gently rubbed her ears.

"Stay, Molly. Stay with Kate." She whimpered when he put her inside.

He backed the Jeep into the barn, muscled his father's shipping crate up and over the tailgate, then drove slowly down the driveway, looking in the rear-view mirror at a house that was still dark.

David woke to full sunlight and a campus parking lot, stiff from sleeping in the driver's seat, his first and only thought, Why? He locked himself in his office, ignored every knock on the door, and finally turned off the lights so no one would know he was there. That evening, he wrote the college a letter of apology and good-bye and left it on his desk.

The next day he drove past the apple orchards west of Sebastopol and past the turnoff to what was now Kate and Molly's place, stopped for gas and groceries in Guerneville, and pushed on through groves of redwoods, out to Jenner, where the Russian River empties into the Pacific.

He found a secluded campsite at Salt Point State Park, pitched his tent to face the sea, walked along a broad marine terrace to Stump Beach, and sat for hours on a driftwood log. He'd introduced Kate to Salt Point, its coves, tide pools, honeycombed rocks. She'd said, laughing and in wonder, "How did you find this place?"

David camped for five days and talked to no one. Each morning he set out early, hiking above sea cliffs in thick fog. Each afternoon, the fog lifted and he watched the ocean's endless blue-green swell until sunset. Sleepless nights were spent beside a campfire.

He missed Molly.

He wasn't going back to Kate.

He distilled his pain in lyrics, filling pages in a notebook, his life now a question. Just before sunrise on the sixth day, David drove to the park entrance then north along the coast.

June 30, 1971

Didn't go to graduation. Don't want to see Ian, don't want him to know where I am. Had diploma mailed to me. Staying with Ronald. We did the centerfold together in a magazine. Money! He says films pay more.

11

October 12, 1987
The lawyer said I should burn all my queer (he actually said it!) mag-
azines and the video collection because they could be used against me.
Kept a few photos of one boy.

Miami Herald, October 27, 1988
Assistant School Principal Terminated

Edward Hayes, the assistant principal at Orange Grove Middle School, was fired last night by a unanimous vote of the school board. Hayes had been placed on paid leave after he was accused of touching several male students inappropriately and a parents' group called for his resignation. Hayes did not appear before the board, but his attorney read a prepared statement that many in the audience said was self-serving and far from the apology they had hoped for.

Earlier in the week, a jury of eight men and four women found Hayes guilty of soliciting an undercover police officer for sex in the men's room at the Southern Stallion Lounge.

The school board disqualified Hayes from severance pay and all life insurance, medical, and pension plans. Hayes' attorney said that the board's decision was based on emotion and was unjustifiably harsh, though he is not planning an appeal. Calls to Hayes' home were not returned.

October 28, 1988
I wanted sex. Why is that wrong?

November 14, 1988
Almost out of money. Ronald doesn't answer my letters. No one else to turn to.

December 1, 1988
Got in touch with Jacques at Connection Records. He says we can make a deal for David's songs because he and I were a duo. Jacques thinks an album of new arrangements will be big. He'll find musicians and a singer. I'll overdub the guitar parts. He offered a generous advance on royalties. David is dead and gone anyway.

September 14, 1989
"Plenty Of Time" album is platinum! "Take It From Me" and "Clean Slate" singles went gold! Music money at last! Bought ten acres near Sonoma and will soon build my dream home.

April 3, 1990
Moved in to my new house! My own design, small but private and luxurious. Overlooks my vineyard. Finally have my place in the country. Got a puppy for company. She loves me.

April 18, 1990
Edward! Why won't you answer my letters? Ronald

May 1, 1990
I am rich. Now what?

May 4, 1990
Edward! Please, please, please. I am sick. I need money for medicine. Remember, I love you very much. Ronald

May 12, 1990
Never forget, Sweetheart: I took your cherry and you were Oh! So! Willing! I am the only friend you've ever had! I have been good to you! Even though you never paid back the money I loaned you! Please. Ronald

June 1, 1990
How can you ignore me? I'm sick! I need medicine! Refuse and you'll regret it! I know how you got your money. Ronald

June 5, 1990
You don't care about anyone but yourself! That's why people don't like you! That's why you're alone! Adieu, Edward. I hate you! Ronald

June 30, 1990
Mr. Hayes —
I am sorry to inform you that Ronald Palmieri died at 3 a.m. yesterday of AIDS. He had asked that I notify you. T. Jorgenson, MSW, San Francisco General Hospital

July 19, 1990
Bored. Started giving music lessons just for something to do. It's good to be teaching again. My HIV test was negative.

12

Sitka, Alaska, August 1, 1990.

Josh Copeland, age seven, said, "We want to go on the *Annie C.*"

"Next week," David said. "For your birthday. Then we'll come back home for your party."

Toby Copeland, Josh's younger brother by two years, said, "Can we steer the boat?"

"Yes, you can steer."

"Can we catch fish?"

"Yes, you can catch fish."

"Are you coming to karate class with me?"

"No, champ. I've got to work. Mom's driving you."

"Come with us," Annie said.

"There's some welding to do and it's time for new injectors. I'll be on the boat all day. Okay, guys, into the Jeep."

Toby said, "Will you tell us the bear story again?"

"Sure. After dinner. We'll sit on the couch and I'll tell you about the bear that came into my tent."

"And the story about the moose?"

"And the story about the moose."

Josh said, "I want to go in the truck."

"Tomorrow we'll go in the truck. Okay, hugs and a handshake for dad. Be good, snug up your seatbelts, and listen to your mom. She loves you both. I do, too."

"See you later," Annie said. "Love you."

David watched the Jeep until it reached the end of the driveway.

In the *Annie C's* engine room, he torqued the last bolts on the valve covers, started the engines, and listened. Satisfied, he wiped his hands clean and went up on deck for some fresh air. He heard sirens in the distance, but didn't turn on the scanner. He looked west toward Mt. Edgecumbe, where he and Annie first noticed each other.

It had been a Wednesday in September, nine years earlier. At dawn, he'd tossed a daypack into his Jeep, borrowed a friend's Zodiac, and set out across Sitka Sound, headed for Kruzof Island.

The water that day reflected a clear sky and the red cone of Mt. Edgecumbe free of snow and fog. He looked forward to the final ascent, a steep walk-up, but for now bald eagles screamed, soared, and cartwheeled overhead and sea otters rested in kelp beds. He turned the throttle down. Why hurry? It was only ten miles to the island.

A black dorsal fin appeared, then others. David shut off the outboard and drifted while two groups of orcas swam near. Blow. Backdive. Sideroll. Belly flop. Tail slap. Breach. A juvenile circled the Zodiac, spyhopping, close enough to touch, eye to eye.

There were no boats moored in the cove at Fred's Creek Cabin and no other hikers at the trailhead. David followed the Mt. Edgecumbe trail through rainforest, over boardwalks and muskeg, up to the tree line. From there, he climbed to the volcano's pumice-capped summit, the crater rim, and views west over the Gulf of Alaska, east to Sitka and Baranoff Island, north to the rhyolite domes that form Crater Ridge. It would have been nice to share it all with someone. Where was she? When would he find her?

When would she find him? He stayed for an hour, chose a lump of obsidian for his rock collection, and started down.

At the edge of a muskeg meadow he stood aside to let three women pass on the trail. One was Sitka's new librarian.

A glance. A smile. He turned to look back. She'd done the same.

David stopped by the library twice that week, checked out books he wasn't going to read, learned her name, and stumbled into asking her for a date. After dinner, they talked for hours. She said, "I was hurt. I don't want to ever go through that again." David said, "We're in the same boat."

Soon they were seeing a lot of each other. On Annie's days off they went sea kayaking. They took long hikes in damp forests. There were nights at her apartment in town, slow dancing. Weekends at his cabin, reading by the fire and cooking together in the kitchen. Christmas at her place, New Year's Eve at his. In February she surprised him with a Valentine's Day card. In March they flew to Connecticut to visit her mother. Annie told him, "She likes you." In April he brought her to a slip at the ANB Harbor and said, "Meet the *Sitka Star*, a fifteen-year-old double-rig trawler. Sixty feet long, steel hull, nearly-new Detroit diesels. She needs a refit, but she's got good bones. I'm buying her. Would you marry a man who owns a fishing boat?"

"I've been thinking that if the boat owner didn't ask me soon I was going to ask him."

On their honeymoon, she said that being with him felt right, that everything in her life had, at last, fallen into place. David understood. He wasn't alone anymore.

He studied commercial fishing and walked himself through the refit, installing new electrical and hydraulic systems, nets, and lifting tackle. When Annie had time, she pitched in. Smeared with paint or oil, she would smile and say, "I'd forgotten how good it feels to put on grubbies and get my hands dirty." They mapped their future and went into business as Copeland Oceanic Commercial Fishing, Incorporated.

One evening in late spring David picked her up at the library. They drove to the harbor and walked along the wharf.

She said, "Why is our masthead light on?"

"I don't know."

"My funny husband. I think you do."

The cabin lights came up. Friends yelled, "Surprise! Happy birthday, Annie!" After dinner, cake, and candles, everyone danced on the afterdeck. David's gift was a portrait he'd drawn while she slept. Annie said, "I will always cherish this. I will always cherish you."

David said, "Look at the stern."

He'd changed the boat's name to *Annie C*. They broke a bottle of champagne over the bow.

David learned where fish ran and when, became known for bringing in a quality catch, and won contracts with upscale markets and restaurants in Seattle and Vancouver. A German pharmaceuticals firm, aware of his background in biology—he would know, they said, where to find certain marine species—placed orders that doubled Copeland Oceanic's earnings. He and Annie began to think about buying a second boat. She worked at the library until Josh was born. Two years after that, Toby came along. David kept photos of them in the wheelhouse, but he didn't need reminders, he knew who he was working for. Annie liked to say that there were no storms the family couldn't weather. Anchored by her love, he was as free as he'd ever been.

Nine years, he thought. Nine very good years. He was grateful for the way things had turned out. Kate Anderson only crossed his mind from time to time.

The work done, David wheeled his tool chest to the truck. He looked again at Mt. Edgecumbe and back at the *Annie C*. Then he noticed the police car parked nearby and John Amory, a friend, waiting.

"David."

"John. What's up?"

"Sit down, Bro."

The sirens. David knew. He just knew. "All three?"

"David, I'm . . ."

"All three, John?"

"All three. I'm sorry. I know it doesn't help, but I am truly sorry."

"How?"

"Tommy Stanza, drunk as a skunk again in his pickup. He hit them head-on, about a mile from your place."

"Where are they?"

"You don't want to see. Think of them as they were."

"Where, John?"

"The morgue. I'll come with you but I don't think you should . . ."

"I *should* have been with them."

The first weeks were the worst. He closed off the rest of the house, lived in the great room, slept on the couch, stared through the windows at Mt. Edgecumbe. Annie loved the view and he'd sited their home to take advantage of it. "Another gift," she'd said, "from my wonderful husband, who I love." He brought out his guitar case for the first time in years but didn't have the heart to open it. He tried watching television, but TV had never interested him and it didn't interest him now. He took the set to the foot of his driveway and put a sign on it: *Free*. He stopped shaving. Let his hair grow long. When friends dropped by he didn't answer the door. When they called he didn't pick up the phone. He went out for groceries late at night so he would see as few people as possible, though everyone knew, of course. The whole town had attended the funeral. "Whatever we can do to help," neighbors said. "Always a place for you at the dinner table, David." "Call if you need to talk."

The insurance settlements came. He didn't open the envelopes for six months. His agent finally asked if he intended to cash the checks and David went to the bank. What did the money mean? Still, it felt good to get out of the house and for the tellers to ask how he was, and he began to visit the *Annie C* and talk shop with other fishermen. He took up jogging and drove into town just to be near people. He drew comfort from sidewalk conversations and friendly waves from passing trucks. At a bookstore, the owner, one of many Sitka women who hoped to become the new Mrs. David Copeland, said, "Hi, stranger. How are you doing?"

"Better, I guess. How's the world treating you?"

"Can't complain. My divorce is final and the bastard moved to Ohio."

"Who's that on the tape player?"

"Ryan Scott. He did "Plenty Of Time," "Nothing Personal," "Read The Fine Print," and "Don't Let It Stop You." They've all been monster hits in the Lower 48. We've got his cassette if you want it. David? David? Are you all right? You don't look well."

"I'll take a cassette."

"You should go home and get some rest. Call me if you need … I'm available."

David pushed the cassette into his truck's deck, listened, then slammed a fist on the steering wheel. Three faded snapshots dropped from the dashboard to the floor. Annie. Josh. Toby. They'd been gone for nine months.

The tape played on.

David hit the wheel again, turned the cassette box over, read the liner notes, studied the label. *Connection Records, Los Angeles. All Songs Copyright Edward Hayes.* That son of a bitch, he thought. That thieving son of a bitch.

At home that night, David lifted his guitar from its case. The songs were still perfect, still complete, still alive. Kate and Molly were memories. He couldn't bring Annie and the boys back. There might be one thing he could set right.

He wrote to attorneys in Los Angeles and found one who was interested in his situation, bought an airline ticket, then realized that a few days wouldn't matter to a man who was in no rush to get there or come home. Why not ride Alaskan and Canadian ferries to Vancouver Island? Camp. Drive the Washington-Oregon-California coast. Stay in hotels when he felt like it. A road trip and a month or more away from Sitka might do him good.

He called his crew down to the *Annie C*, gave them generous severance checks, and told them he was sorry. He visited a friend and asked him to keep an eye on the house and the boat and to bring in his mail. David said he didn't know when he'd be back. They shook hands. The friend said, "I'll see you when I see you."

David lifted his shipping crate into the truck bed and pried open the lid. Old flannel shirts lined the bottom. He layered in books and clothing, padlocked the hasp, then packed his tent, sleeping bag, camp stove, and tools around the crate. Two duffle bags and the guitar case filled the rear seat.

A final walk through the house.

A stop at the memorial park, where he sat beside a grave and touched the stone.

Annie Gates-Copeland
May 23, 1951 — August 1, 1990
Toby Davidson Copeland
October 29, 1985 — August 1, 1990
Josh Michael Copeland
August 8, 1983 — August 1, 1990
David Michael Copeland
November 9, 1948 —

Too early, David waited at the Sitka ferry terminal for three hours. When the hull doors opened, he drove onto a Sitka-Prince Rupert ferry. Parked on the automobile deck. Collected his cabin key from the purser. Locked the guitar case and duffels in his cabin and climbed the stairs to the sun deck, where campers pitched tents as he had on his first trip north, and other passengers crowded the rail. College students. Chattering families. Quiet, older couples. Young men under heavy backpacks going or having gone into the wild. A woman alone, about his age, looking at him, liking what she saw. He stayed just long enough to watch Sitka fade into the fog, tried to read in his cabin, but fell asleep. He woke near midnight, found a lounge chair on an upper deck and slept under a clearing sky.

In Prince Rupert, Canadian Customs asked if he had any loaded weapons to declare. He said, truthfully, that he did not.

On the Prince Rupert-Port Hardy ferry, David ate by himself in the cafeteria and listened to groups of tourists loudly admire fjords, glaciers, snow-covered peaks, and forests descending to the sea. All too familiar. He wasn't on vacation. His inside passage was just one leg of a business trip. He went to his stateroom, passed the day reading, and thought that he might stop in Port Hardy for a day or two. But the town reminded him of Sitka and he drove south.

Over the next week he camped out of the truck, moving every day, choosing only isolated sites. Mountain view, lake view, ocean view, it didn't matter. But now solitude—his old friend—came with a price. Now, alone and lonely were one and the same. Now, the Milky Way, a campfire, and distant, howling wolves weren't enough.

He caught an evening ferry from Victoria to Port Angeles. Out in open water, the ship began to pitch and roll as it beat its way through strong winds on the Strait of Juan de Fuca. Passengers huddled inside, the rough crossing too much for them. David stood at the bow, tears and rain falling together while the lights of Port Angeles grew closer.

Port Angeles.

Kate.

She had grown up just south of town, on her mother's farm.

He checked into a downtown motel, unpacked, then pulled the local phone directory from a dresser drawer. Maybe Kate had come back. Maybe . . . No. He went out, walking streets she must have known as a girl. He knew he shouldn't look in the phone-book. He knew he would.

Her name.

Her phone number.

Her address.

In the morning, he shaved, went out, dozed for two hours on a bench at the waterfront park, stopped in for a haircut. It was mid-afternoon before he wrote down the address and took it to the front desk.

"That's the Anderson farm," said the clerk. "Go down Black Diamond Road about three miles. Look for a signpost with a bunch of names and arrows."

Signpost. Hand-lettered name: *K. Anderson*. Gravel driveway that curved toward a farmstead. Chicken coops. Fenced vegetable garden. Tin-roofed house, clapboard siding weathered to gray. Screened porch. Raised flower beds in the front yard. Older station wagon, tags current, tires worn. A once-red barn. Music inside the house loud and familiar, an album he'd given her years ago. No lyrics, just guitars, bass, drums. David knocked softly several times, waited, and knocked again, hard.

"Just a minute, damnit!" Kate's voice. Then she was opening the door. Her house smelled of herbs, flowers, and bread fresh from the oven.

She looked away, then back at him. "No. Oh, no. You're not really here . . . I was thinking about you a minute ago." She reached out to touch his jacket and said, "You *are* here."

"Hi. You still take my breath away."

"I don't understand . . . I don't know why you . . . Oh, hold me. Just . . . hold me."

"I've been thinking about you and I finally realized that I wanted to see you. Thought I'd stay in the area for a day or two."

"Stay here. I've got lots of room. There's no one else around. How did you find me?"

"Small town."

"Come in. Come on in."

"Hey, who's your buddy?"

"That's Mitchell, the purebred Australian Shepherd farm dog. Mitch for short."

"Does he ever move?"

"He moves fast when raccoons come around and he learns fast. It only took one skunk. You remember *that*, don't you, Mitch?"

Tail flop. Yawn.

"If someone comes to the house, Mitch settles on his dog bed.

He's too lazy to bark or get up to say hello. He'll come over for ear rubs when he's ready."

"You're back on your family's homestead."

"When mom passed away, my sister and I inherited the house and twenty-five acres free and clear. We talk about turning it into a working farm again, but she has a good job with the state and isn't interested, so here I am. I love this old place, especially the living room."

The living room. Window seat, brick fireplace, furnishings sturdy, country-like and comfortable, the kind of home, David thought, they'd have made for themselves if . . .

His old stereo.

His old records.

His old photographs crowded together on the mantel, all familiar, all in matching frames. There he was, twenty years younger. And Kate, also younger. And Molly.

"She wouldn't eat or chase tennis balls in the orchard anymore," Kate said. "She just lay by the front door. She died there one night, waiting for you."

"Who is this? He looks like you."

"My son, James David Anderson. He earned a full scholarship, otherwise he'd be working in a paper mill instead of going to college. He wants to be a doctor."

"Good kid."

"He is, and I should know. He was born in this house. I raised him all by myself, and he's my best friend."

"How are you?"

"Okay. I get by on part-time waitress pay, tips, food stamps, my garden, and my chickens. I'm used to money being tight. I don't have anything new, but I've found that I don't need much. I don't even own a TV."

"You look good."

"I . . ."

"Hey, I never saw you blush before."

"I'll be okay in a minute . . . There. Dinner will be garden salad, roast chicken, homemade biscuits. Sorry I can't offer you any wine. I don't drink anymore and I don't keep alcohol around. I swore off everything after I became pregnant with James. Would you start a fire? We can eat in the living room."

Strawberries for dessert. A long, slow evening. Dishes washed and put away. The fire burning low.

Kate said, "Come to bed."

"I didn't drop by to . . ."

"I know. Come to bed."

"We're older, Kate. We can't change things. We can't go back."

"We're not *too* old. Let go of the past."

"It's been a long time."

"For me, too. Let go of the past. Take off your clothes. Come to bed."

David lay down beside her, their bodies together, every move and touch remembered, as if they had never been apart.

Kate said, "I have missed you so much."

After breakfast Kate said, "Mitch and I like to sit on the back porch swing and look at the Olympic Mountains. Sit with us."

"Million dollar view."

"The Olympics always remind me how you used to say mountains don't know we're here and that everything's connected, on up to the stars. Now tell me what you did after you left."

"Quit school. Resigned my teaching post."

"School and teaching were your life."

"*You* were my life."

"You were hardly ever home with *me*."

"I was building our future. I thought we both understood."

"You said you loved me."

"I meant it."

"But you didn't come back."

"How could I? I was angry, disappointed, devastated."

"Will you ever forgive me?"

"I did, Kate. Years ago. But some things are always going to hurt."

"We were good together."

"Then why? Why? You knew I'd ask when you opened the front door."

"I'll never know. That guy, I didn't care about him. We got high a few times, then he said, 'Do you want to fix, it's great.' You came home early."

Neither spoke for a while, then Kate said, "Where did you go?"

"North, up the coast, as far as Sitka. I was just settling in when I got drafted. I told them I wanted to serve as a medic and they said okay. I put my things in storage, left my Jeep and the Martin with a friend and went."

David stood to stretch his legs, patted Mitch on the head, and leaned on the porch rail.

"There was a guy in my platoon, Glenn Siegel. He and I were close, like brothers. We talked about life, guitars, philosophy. He wanted to start a blues band, get married, earn a PhD in physics, join the space program, walk on the moon. You'd have liked him.

"A week before Glenn's tour was up, the Viet Cong attacked our base. A mortar round killed two men and tore Glenn's right leg off at the hip. I crawled over to do what I could, but he died just as I got to him. A sniper kept shooting at his body, turning it into hamburger. Well, I could see the sniper. I knew he could see me. I mean, we looked right at each other. I don't know why he didn't kill me. I got mad and shot him with Glenn's M16, then I shot every VC I saw. Couldn't say how many."

David paused and sat down.

"I stayed mad and volunteered for sniper training. They sent me to sniper school then back to my unit."

"Killing people. That's not like you."

"It wasn't. Until somebody blew my friend's leg off and shot the rest of him to pieces."

"What does it feel like?"

"Like nothing. You think, 'They're dead, I'm not.' You move on. After I got out I headed back to Sitka. Tried to forget Vietnam, but no one who was there can do that. I worked on fishing boats. Built a cabin. Lived alone. Backpacked, hunted, cut firewood, watched the northern lights. Wrote songs, did a lot of reading. Annie Gates and I found each other. We got married. Had two boys."

"Where is she? Where are your kids?"

"Dead. All dead, last year."

"Oh, David."

"She was driving home and a drunk hit them. The police said he was doing seventy in a thirty-five zone. It was his third DUI."

"How awful."

"It was. Is."

"Be straight with me, David. What are you doing here?"

"Come out to the truck."

The truck, a GMC Jimmy that had been through many winters. Alaska license plate. Paint faded, interior clean but cluttered. Duffle bags. Camping gear. Guitar case. David's treasured shipping crate in the back. Cassette tapes on the console. Snapshots in a cup holder.

David said, "Annie. Josh. Toby."

"I don't know what to say."

"There's nothing to say." He placed the pictures in the glove box, locked its door shut, and slid a cassette into the player.

"Your songs! I heard them on the radio and wondered why you weren't singing."

"I didn't record or license them. Jacques and Edward did. They don't have the rights."

"What will you do?"

"Talk to an attorney in Los Angeles."

"And then what?"

"Find the little thief."

"I need to tell you something about Ian."

Kate's phone rang early the next morning and she ran to answer it.

"I thought it might be James. I have to go to work. I'll be home this afternoon. If you want to look through them, your things are in the barn. Books, clothes, photos, drawings, Nevermore, Mr. R."

"Maybe after I'm done in California we can spend some time together and figure things out."

"I'd like that."

"Me too."

David was gone when Kate returned. An envelope that contained $5,000 and a note was on the kitchen table: *Use the money as you wish. Please hold onto the Martin for me and keep it in its case and in the house. I left my shipping crate in the barn. I took the lock off.*

13

David drove along the coast, reversing his old northward path. He knew the roads, the beaches, the scenery. No need for maps, no need to stop at Salt Point, no need to turn east into Sonoma County, back toward the college, 805 Grove Street, and the house on Apple Tree Road. Better to keep heading south—past Bodega Bay, through Marin County then San Francisco, Monterey, Carmel—and camp in the hills above Big Sur.

Los Angeles.

Smog, traffic, crowds, generic hotel room, a meeting with an attorney who asked how he liked Southern California.

David sat in the front office at Connection Records for an hour before the receptionist said, "Jacques will see you now."

Jacques. Gold necklace, gold earrings, gold phone, gold and platinum records on the walls. Hands out of sight, he sat behind a massive desk and said, "Edward told me you were dead."

"Do I look dead?"

"Tell me why you're here. I don't know why you're here."

"Don't play it small, Jacques. I wrote the songs."

"That will be difficult for you to prove, I don't care how many attorneys you hire. You've already been to see one, right? We copyrighted everything in Edward's name and we can tie you up in court for years. You don't have a chance."

"Where is he?"

"Are you nuts, David? I won't tell you that. Get out."

"Where is Ed?"

"Get the hell out. Hey. Hey! Let go of me!"

"Where is he? Tell me or I'll break your arm."

"Okay! Okay! He lives near Sonoma. Jesus! Here's his address."

"Give me yours, too."

"Why?"

"Give it. Show me your driver's license. You don't want me to learn that you called him."

David drove north, away from Los Angeles, up and over the Grapevine on an interstate heavy with truck traffic. Drove with his windows open to a warm Central Valley night. Drove almost without seeing the highway. Drove and replayed the past.

Edward: "We'll have money, more than we ever dreamed of."

Annie: "I will always cherish you."

Josh: "We want to go on the *Annie C.*"

Toby: "Will you tell us the bear story again?"

Molly the happy dog, barking her joy to see him.

What Kate told him about Ian.

He pulled into a rest area, punched a duffle into a pillow, and slept over the steering wheel. In the morning, he bought newspapers and a shower at a truck stop and made his way through the knot of congested Bay Area freeways, then along uncrowded two-lane roads to a small vineyard outside Sonoma.

———————

Sometimes, the doorbell startled Edward. If he wasn't looking out a front window, if Sandy didn't bark, if he was busy with a video, he couldn't tell that a vehicle had come up the drive. But today he was expecting new videos from Jacques, by special courier. He opened his front door, jumped back and said, "You're not dead!"

"No."

"What do you want?"

"To talk. Can I come in?"

"Ah . . . for a few minutes. I have . . . someone coming over. We'll talk in my studio. It's back here."

"You still have your old Martin."

"They'll bury it with me."

"Nice studio, nice house. You've done well with my songs."

"*Our* songs!"

"I wrote them."

"*I* gave them to the world!"

"They weren't *yours* to give! You stole them. And those lamps. You stole them, too. They were in your room at 805 Grove Street. They belonged to Ian. By the way, did you see? Ian's in the paper. The Society pages."

"I saw. Who cares?"

"No one *cares*, Ed, except Ian. When was the last time *you* were in the paper?"

"What do you mean by that?"

"Did you know he raped Kate?"

"No, but so what? She broke us up! We could have been big!"

"I didn't want to be big."

"Is this about money?"

"Simple honesty, something you've never understood. You're going to tell the world that you're a thief and that the songs are rightfully mine. We'll be in *Rolling Stone* again. Connection Records, too. And Jacques."

"You'll never make me do it."

"This house, the vineyard, you didn't earn them. They're not really yours. They'll be taken away and you and your dog will have to leave."

"*You* leave! Get out of my house! *My* house! I don't want you here!"

———————

Late that afternoon, David parked across the street from 805 Grove. The concrete driveway was still pushed up and broken by tree roots, the house still needed a paint job and a new roof. Twenty years on, no one had bothered to fix the front stairs. Twenty years ago, he would have never thought he'd see the place again. It was a house you lived in for a while, left, and forgot. Now, far from his life in Sitka, he woke up angry every day, his first thoughts Ian and what had happened in the old Victorian. And Edward.

Sitting in his truck the next morning, he reread Ian's newspaper profile.

Still the same . . . my little empire . . . I leave my office every afternoon at exactly 4:45.

I time the traffic lights so I won't have to stop.

What did Ian say long ago at the warehouse? Something about Lee Harvey Oswald.

May 10, 1991
David is alive! Came here today. I called Jacques as soon as he left. How did David find me? Jacques says he doesn't know.

May 11, 1991
Can't sleep. Don't know what David will do.

———————————

May 13, 1991.

Park in an alley behind the Hamilton warehouse. Climb the fire escape. Crowbar open a rusted fire door on the fourth floor, Ian's floor. Same dim light, same smell of mold, same dust, same old furniture, same old shotgun case. Camp stool. Binoculars. Cut through thick layers of paint and raise a window. Watch the lobby door two buildings up from the intersection of Mission and 1st. A two-day recon, an hour a day, was all he would need. David checked his watch: 4:45. Four minutes later, Ian appeared, herringbone jacket slung over a shoulder, the same longish blonde hair, his walk still an arrogant shuffle. He reached the corner just as the light turned green.

May 14, 1991.

Ian came out at 4:51 and stood at the corner, nervous and fidgeting, for a long light, exactly 50 seconds by David's watch. Perfect. He saw himself taking the shot, saw how it would go from set-up to follow-through, his shooting platform a beanbag on the window sill. Load and insert the magazine. Slide the bolt forward and down. Release thumb safety, weld cheek to stock, breathe in then out, line up the sights, compensate for the downhill angle and the bullet drop. Breathe in again then out, squeeze the trigger, breathe in then out. Standard stuff, and he'd engaged harder targets. Here, there were no VC and no probing fire. No ever-present mosquitoes. No snakes, no wet, tropical heat that he couldn't get used to, no stench of mud and rotting vegetation, no leeches inside his clothing. But think, think hard. What could go wrong? What if Ian was with someone tomorrow?

May 15, 1991.

David sat at the window, ready. At 4:55 Ian and a woman walked to the corner arm in arm. They stopped for the light. He let go of her arm. The light changed. Ian didn't move.

Breathe in, breathe out, aim. In, out, squeeze. Breathe in, breathe out, add a follow-up shot just because. Breathe in, breathe out.

The woman began to scream.

Two days later.

Edward thought, Why wouldn't David leave him alone? What was done was done and David should accept it, but here he was again, getting out of his truck, talking to Sandy, petting her like she was his, carrying a briefcase.

Edward said, "If there's something in there you think I'll sign, I won't. Sandy! Here!"

"My last visit to you ever, Ed. I promise. Talk in your studio?"

"I'll give you five minutes. No more."

Yesterday's newspapers were spread across Edward's desk. He said, "Ian."

"Made the front page this time."

"Who would do that to him?"

"Someone who wanted to get even, I guess." David opened his briefcase. "Anything more to say about your bed buddy the rapist before we get down to business?"

"Kate parked her ass on his bed and *begged* him for it! *That's* what I have to say! Now go away! There's no business to get down to! I won't sign anything!"

"You won't have to."

14

Joe said, "How's the research going, Ben?"

"I'm still hunting for the woman, but I've found the other roommate in the photo. David Michael Copeland, born 1948 in San Francisco. Lived at 805 Grove Street from May 1970 until April 1971. Rising star in biology, dropped out when he almost had his Master's. U.S. Army, 1972-1973, Vietnam, one tour. Went in as a medic, came out as a sniper. Twenty-three confirmed kills. Honorable discharge. He's been in Alaska ever since."

"Medic to sniper? That's unusual. Where in Alaska?"

"Sitka. Know anybody up there?"

"Turns out I do. John Amory, old army buddy. He's with the Sitka Police Department. Let's call him."

"Yes," John Amory said, "I know David Copeland. Everyone in town knows David. He's a good friend and a good man. Owns a beautiful fishing boat, the *Annie C.* His wife and their two boys were killed last year. Car wreck."

Ben said, "Any idea where Copeland might be?"

"Haven't seen him lately. I'll ask around and get back to you."

After lunch at Jake's, Ben said, "Joe, I'm going up there. I'll catch a red-eye to Vancouver then a flight to Sitka and see if I can get a search warrant for Copeland's property. Be back in a couple days."

"Wild goose chase?"

"More research. I have a feeling about this."

At the Sitka airport, John Amory said, "Welcome to Sitka, Ben. Judge Littlefield wants to see you right away."

In her chambers the judge said, "You've come 1,500 miles, Deputy Hyatt. Tell me and John what we need to know."

"First off," Ben said, "I may want to collect evidence and take it with me."

John Amory drove through Sitka, then away from town along Halibut Point Road.

Ben said, "Beautiful scenery."

"I wake up to it every day. Don't know how I got so lucky."

"How long until we get to Copeland's place?"

"We'll be there in five minutes." Amory pulled off the road. "Right here's where Annie and the boys died. A head-on. The driver was a piece of crap named Tony Stanza. He blew point one-nine and couldn't even stand up to do it. I went down to the boat to tell David, hardest thing I've ever done. He and Annie were real popular and some folks wanted to lynch Stanza, so we kept him in jail. He got an attorney. We had to let him out."

"What happened?"

"He disappeared. David had an airtight alibi, but I've always thought that Stanza went off the *Annie C* into some very deep water, probably way out in the Gulf of Alaska."

"And Copeland?"

"I didn't see David for some time. Then there he was in town one day, talking, starting to heal."

"I don't know how a man could come back from that."

"I couldn't. How do you forget?"

"Or forgive."

"When he and Annie got married, David designed and built a log home. Real craftsmanship, you'll see. It was in an architectural magazine. He drives a 1970 Ford long-bed pickup that looks like it never left the showroom. Does all the work on his boat. He can repair anything or fabricate anything. The guy's a natural."

Amory parked in David's driveway, got out of the cruiser, and said, "Best if you let me do this. It'll be easier if it comes from me." Right hand on his sidearm, Ben watched Amory peer into the garage then go to the front door.

"His truck is gone, Ben. There's no one home. The door's not locked. Let's go in."

In David's office, they found unopened mail and an unlocked gun safe.

"Two calibers of interest to you in there, Ben. One box of .45 ACP and one of 9mm Luger. Also a box of 7.62x51mm NATO. No guns. Lots of old black-and-white photographs. People, mostly. Soldiers. This one says, 'Normandy, June 1944.' The officer wearing a beret looks like David Copeland."

"Probably his father. What's that short rifle in his hand?"

"De Lisle Commando Carbine, I'll bet. Mean anything to you?"

"No."

"Maybe it's what you're looking for. A friend of mine built a replica. We'll drive out to his place and he'll tell you all about De Lisles."

———

At Jakes, Ben said, "I fired the replica, Joe. Quieter than a BB gun, no recoil, no muzzle flash. It's really unbelievable. Oh . . . this photograph: David Copeland's wife and kids."

"Lucky man. For a few years."

"His father was Michael Davidson Copeland, Captain, Royal Marine Commandos. Born 1919. Left his music studies at Cambridge

University in 1938 and joined the Army. Volunteered for the British Commandos in 1941. Sniper. Led raids in Norway and France. Wounded March 1942. Recovered. Became an instructor at the Royal Marine Commando School. Led more raids. Went ashore on D-Day. Fought in France, the Netherlands, and Germany. Distinguished Conduct Medal, Conspicuous Gallantry Medal, Military Cross."

"Quite a guy."

"Thirty-nine confirmed kills by early 1944. Kept a sort of diary. I found it in Copeland's house."

> *3 March 1944. Issued De Lisle silenced carbine. Marvelous gun.*
> *8 March 1944. #40. First Jerry with the De Lisle.*
> *15 May 1944. Sentry. #41. De Lisle.*
> *16 May 1944. Sentry. #42. DL.*
> *17 May 1944. Sentry. #43, DL.*
> *6, 7, 8, 9 June 1944. Bren Gun. No idea how many Jerries, so stopped counting.*
> *10 June 1944. Sentry. DL.*
> *11 June 1944. Sentry. DL.*
> Ben said, "No entries for eight months."
> *2 February 1945. Nicked a Belgian Browning Hi-Power from a storeroom. Have idea for a suppressor. Will need a threaded barrel.*
> *21 April 1945. Barrel (unauthorised) not an easy work-up.*
> *5 May 1945. HP barrel finished. Suppressor perfect.*
> *6 May 1945. Oberstleutnant. HP. Unofficial.*
> *7 May 1945. SS-Obersturmfuhrer. HP. Unofficial.*

"Then the war ended. Copeland married an American nurse in 1946, emigrated to the U.S., and became a naturalized citizen. She died of lung cancer when David was five; he died in 1967. Here's a photo of him holding a De Lisle."

"Strange looking little thing."

"Clever, though. Straight out of World War II England, where everything was scarce. To make De Lisles, the Brits scrounged old Lee-Enfield rifles, bored the .303 receivers out to .45 ACP, then added cut-down Thompson submachine gun barrels and modified Colt M1911 pistol magazines. An integral suppressor covered the whole barrel. Working the bolt was louder than firing the weapon. John's friend said it's probably the quietest firearm ever made."

"Why .45? That's a pistol round."

"It's slow and subsonic. Easier to suppress than a faster bullet. But it hits hard."

"You can't hear the shot?"

"No. Only about 129 were built between 1943 and 1945, but a buzz bomb destroyed the factory and the production records, so, officially, no one knows. De Lisles weren't given to regular army units, just commandos, mostly for sentry removal on raids, headshots being the preferred method. A sentry would just drop and the Germans couldn't figure out where the bullet came from. Officers were also a favorite target. De Lisles are accurate to about 200 yards."

"How far from the warehouse window to Hamilton's head?"

"Thirty-five yards. There's no way to tell how many original De Lisles are still around or how many replicas have been made. I think we're looking for an original and I think David Copeland got it from his father."

"And the stolen Belgian Hi-Power . . ."

"Could be our 9mm."

15

Ben held The Photo, as he'd come to think of it: 805 Grove Street. Front porch. Four people. "It's all here, Joe. Everything that passed between the roommates."

"Is that Hayes' smashed guitar?"

"I think so. And I can't tell, but the gun on Hamilton's lap is probably half of his matched pair. At some point he took it back to the warehouse."

"I'll vote for that."

"Copeland's old girlfriend was easy to find. She lives in Port Angeles, Washington. She's single, she's on welfare, and she might know where Copeland is."

"It's worth a try."

"We'll fly to Seattle, drive to Port Angeles, run a few things by a judge and the local sheriff, then check in with Kate Anderson's social worker and eligibility supervisor, Mrs. Carol Walters."

A voice on the intercom. "Carol, two police officers from California to see you about Kate Anderson."

"Give me a minute."

As she always did when visitors came to her office, Carol Walters took her family photographs off the shelves and put them in a desk drawer. She paused with her favorite, a silver-framed portrait of Katie. So many years gone by, and so quickly. Katie would soon be 42 and she, herself, was already 43, hard to believe. The intercom cut in on her thoughts. "Carol?" She placed the portrait face-down on her desk, pressed the intercom button, and said, "Send them in."

Joe said, "Mrs. Walters, I am Inspector Joe D'Alessandro, San Francisco Police Department, and this is Sonoma County Sheriff's Deputy Ben Hyatt. We're investigating two homicides in California. One of your clients, Kate Anderson, is a person of interest. If you would please bring her file."

"Client files are confidential. I think you already know that. You'll need a court order. From Washington. Not California. And a local sheriff to serve it. And I will need time to redact certain private and personal information in her file."

"Well, this *is* a murder investigation. We have . . ."

"I told you. Client files are confidential."

". . . a Washington court order and a sheriff standing by to serve it, but I thought we could be somewhat less formal. Here's a notarized copy for you."

"Is this real?"

"I assure you, Mrs. Walters, it is quite real. I stood in a Seattle courtroom yesterday to explain why I needed it. Do you want me to tell the judge that you've got a problem with his signature?"

"I'll get her file. I'll need a few minutes."

"Take your time, Mrs. Walters. We've got all day."

Joe watched her walk away. "Does she look familiar? I think she looks familiar."

Ben lifted the silver frame and tapped the photograph. *To Sis on her 43rd — Love always, Katie.*

Joe said, "Our lady of the porch."

"Calling Katie . . ."

Joe looked at his watch. "Right about . . . now."

Kate Anderson's thin file—"*Too* thin," Joe said—contained nothing he and Ben didn't already know.

At Kate's front door Joe said, "Farm girl. No doorbell." The door opened.

"Yes?"

"Ms. Anderson," Joe said. "We'd like to ask you a few questions about Edward Hayes, Ian Hamilton, and David Copeland. I believe your sister told you who we are and that we were coming."

"Um . . . Yes . . . Well . . . alright. Come into the living room. It's okay, my dog doesn't bite. I saw the story about Ian on the TV at work. You don't think David had anything to do with it?"

"Edward Hayes was killed two days after Ian Hamilton died."

"Edward? Who would kill Edward? Not David."

"Do you know where he is?"

"No."

"I have to say that if you're hiding anything, anything at all, I can have you charged with obstruction of justice and your sister with fraud. A meeting with her supervisor will only be the beginning. I don't want to do that, so you'll need to be upfront with me right here and right now. I'm listening."

Ben said, "Please understand, Ms. Anderson. This is your only chance to tell the truth the easy way. Don't try to shield David Copeland. We just want to talk to him."

"Really, I don't know where he is."

"When did you last see him?"

"About four weeks ago. He stayed here for a day and a half. He said Edward stole his songs and he was going to find a lawyer in Los Angeles."

"Did he mention any lawyers' names?"

"No."

Joe said, "You all lived in the same house. Tell us about it. Start with Edward Hayes."

"Those little grey eyes. He just stared at you. And his short, curly hair. Back then, most guys wore it long. Edward was different. Moody. Always upset about one thing or another. Sometimes he didn't talk to us for a whole day. It seemed like he couldn't get along with anyone and David often said that Edward couldn't get along with himself. I think he was only happy when he was playing his guitar. He and David played and sang in bars, but only songs David wrote. Edward wanted to record the songs. David didn't."

"I'm guessing that you and Mr. Copeland lived together in California?"

"Twenty years ago. We broke up. I moved here."

"Did he say why he came to see you after all this time?"

"He said he'd been thinking about me."

Joe said, "Ian Hamilton?"

"Oh. Him."

———————

Ian Hamilton was in a hurry to collect his mail and laundry then drive to the city for an evening with Joanna.

He took the stairs at 805 Grove Street two at a time and opened the front door, greeted by loud psychedelic music. He yelled, "Turn it down!" He walked along the hall to David and Kate's room and opened their door. Shades drawn. Rolling papers strewn about. Empty wine bottles next to David's easy chair. Kate face down on the unmade bed, out cold. She was beautiful, no doubt about it. Ian turned the stereo off, returned to his room, picked up his laundry bags, set them down. He thought, She doesn't know I'm here,

Edward's gone to San Francisco, David is backpacking somewhere. No one knows I'm here.

He stepped through David and Kate's doorway, leaned over the bed, pushed her skirt over her waist. Lord, what a body.

She whispered, "David."

Ian said, "Right here."

He'd wanted this from the first moment he saw her. He'd waited months. He unzipped his pants, knelt behind Kate. Then he was inside, moving. He heard only his labored breathing, felt only what he wanted to feel, finished, pulled free, stood quickly to close his zipper. That was how he liked it: no resistance, the girl drunk and easy.

"Ms. Anderson," Ben said. "Could it have been anyone else?"

"It had to be Ian. Laundry gone, mail gone, front door locked. His Friday afternoon routine."

"Did you report it? Did you tell anyone?"

"Report it? In those days rape was always the woman's fault. I told my sister. She paid for an abortion while David was away on a field trip. I would never carry Ian's child. I didn't tell David. I got stoned all the time and drank a lot when he wasn't around. Didn't always take my birth control pills. Stupid, I know."

Joe said, "The photographs above your fireplace, Ms. Anderson. Very nice. The young man in the cap and gown. Who is he?"

"My son. I didn't want another abortion."

"Is David Copeland his father?"

"I don't know who his father is."

Ben said, "These of you and Mr. Copeland. Where were they taken?"

"Saline Valley. David loved it. This is at the hot springs, this is a waterfall and swimming hole near our camp. I called it my oasis. These are my petroglyphs. Not *mine*, but we called them that. We were just kids in the desert. That one's our dog, Molly. David bought her for me. She loved tennis balls."

———————

Driving back to the Seattle airport Joe said, "Saline Valley. Where's that?"

"Southern California."

"You know it?"

"Not first-hand. I've heard it's a good place to go if you don't want to be found."

"Anderson's still a beauty. Didn't get far on her looks, though."

"No pictures of her sister."

"Oh, those were taken down before we got there."

"I forgot to ask why she and Copeland called it quits."

"He could be anywhere, Ben."

"I know where he is."

16

David drove on back roads and through small towns, into central Oregon, sleeping in the truck, camping in pine forests. Near Bend, he began to think about the mountains and fault-bounded valleys that lay south and east, the stretched, broken crust of the earth, Basin and Range. East of Burns, he remembered that Kate had been happy in Saline Valley. Why not go there now? See the sun rise over one mountain range and set behind another. Stand under a waterfall in a canyon. Watch the desert do what it does best: nothing. After that? Port Angeles, probably. But sooner or later, wherever he went, somebody would come for him. Why drag Kate into it? He turned around and drove west then south, beneath the Abert Rim, through Alturas, Reno, the Carson Valley and the West Walker River Valley, past Mono Lake, down Sherwin Grade to a side-street motel in Bishop.

He stayed for three days, keeping to himself, reading in his room, walking the town's streets during pre-dawn hours. Afternoons were spent by the motel pool, where he absorbed the crisp warmth of June. On the fourth morning, he packed his duffel bags, filled extra gas cans, checked the tires and bought two mounted spares, and picked up camouflage nets at a surplus store. Next came ice, boxed firewood, groceries, and, on impulse, barbecued chickens—the scraps would be a windfall for coyotes and

Kit foxes. "Listen To Me" played on the market's music system and shadowed him to the checkout. "Hey," David wanted to tell the cashier whisper-singing his words to herself, "Ed Hayes didn't write that. I did."

He mailed a letter to Kate, drove south to Big Pine, then east for two miles to a turnoff and familiar road signs—*No Snow Removal. Travel At Your Own Risk. Pavement Ends*—then south again over patchy snow on Waucoba-Death Valley Road to another sign, weather-beaten and bullet-scarred—*Saline Valley Road, Warning, No Services Available.*

Saline Valley Road. An 80 mile-long washboard hard on the suspension. A lonely, rough-graded bed of gravel and jagged, tire-killing rocks.

David eased the truck down tight switchbacks into Marble Canyon, across Opal Canyon's ruts greasy with brown mud, around hub-deep sand at Whippoorwill Flat, and through snowdrifts atop North Pass. At the mouth of Whippoorwill Canyon he stopped to consider the view and the way forward, a long, straight stretch, downhill all the way. Scattered Joshua trees. Shallow salt lake shining in the sun. Sand dunes in the distance. High wall of the Inyo Mountains to the west, the Saline, Cottonwood, and Last Chance ranges out east. Up ahead, two barricades and two signs. *Road Closed. Washout Ahead.* David drove past the barricades and across a broad channel still damp from a recent flash flood, then back to the road. He pushed on, down and down into Saline Valley, arid basin of sagebrush and salt.

Almost there.

An abandoned jeep trail angled along a draw, crossed a dry creek bed, then disappeared up an alluvial fan. David locked the hubs, engaged the crawler gear, and turned onto the old track.

Fifteen minutes later he topped a rise, dropped behind a low ridge, cut the ignition, and rolled to a stop where he and Kate had camped. It didn't look like anyone had been there since then.

Empty miner's shack. Rust-eaten 1940s dump truck, no hood, seats, doors, or new bullet holes. The stone cairn Kate put up twenty years earlier. The fire ring they'd built together.

When a Kit fox and her pups had wandered into camp, David said, "If we come back next year they'll remember us." When coyotes howled in the distance, he said, "They're telling the world I love you." When an earthquake startled Kate one morning before dawn he told her, "We're safe. The mountains don't know we're here." She looked up at the Milky Way every night and said, "I didn't know there were so many stars," and called a nearby waterfall and its plunge pool her oasis, saying, "Why can't we live here? This is a good place."

A good place. Protected on three sides by overhanging cliffs, the Inyo Mountains at your back, a year-round stream at the mouth of a canyon. Hidden from the main road. Day or night, you'd know if someone came up the draw.

David checked for fields of fire, felt foolish, then told himself it was just an old habit. He parked the truck under a rock ledge, draped the camouflage nets, and pitched his tent with a view toward sunrise. Legs dangling, he sat on the tailgate while shadows swept the valley beneath passing clouds. At dusk he built a fire, set a camp chair by the stone ring, took one of the roast chickens from a deli bag. A Kit fox appeared. David held out a drumstick. The fox crept closer, took the gift from his hand, and scampered into the night.

Campfire thoughts.

Tomorrow would be Kate's birthday. The day after that would mark the twenty-fourth anniversary of his father's death.

After the internment, David sifted through his father's papers and belongings. In a shipping crate, he found his own birth certificate. A saxophone and spare reeds. Family photo albums. The deed to his parents' first house. Their handwritten marriage vows. His mother's wedding dress, wedding ring, and death certificate. His father's war diary, the part of his life he never talked about.

In Alaska, back from Vietnam, he pored over the diary, comparing his war with his father's. A note had been tucked inside the cover: *David—The crate. False bottom, wire loop. Things you might need someday.*

He pulled on the wire loop, pried the bottom up, and found an envelope containing $5,000 in small bills; a Browning semi-automatic pistol and a thread-on suppressor, both caked in Cosmoline and wrapped in soft cotton flannel; a black ordnance box. Inside, a short rifle rested on a felt-lined cradle. A black metal tube made up half the gun's length. Engraved on the tube were the words *The De LIsle Carbine Cal. .45 ACP.*

All the years of lugging the crate around and he hadn't known.

David disassembled the Browning and the suppressor. Degreased, reassembled then oiled and polished, they looked new. He fired the pistol suppressed and without the suppressor. Though he had no use for the handsome weapon, he liked having it around.

He lifted the De Lisle from the box, filled the 7-round magazine, closed the bolt, and fired at a paper target. He felt a mild recoil and smelled burnt gunpowder, but there'd been no loud report, no muzzle flash. What was wrong? He worked the bolt, examined the spent cartridge, squeezed the trigger, again felt an undersized recoil, and heard his bullet slap the bullseye. He clamped the gun to a shooting rest, tied a string to the trigger, and walked off. At twenty-five feet shots were barely audible. Beyond that, he couldn't hear them at all. The De Lisle was quiet by design. He went to a gunsmith and together they took the carbine apart.

"I've heard about these," the smith said. "You've got a rare bird. This tube is basically an integral suppressor. The barrel, which sits inside the tube, is ported, as you can see. Gases from a shot leave the ports and fill the rear of the tube. It's an expansion chamber. Meanwhile, the bullet leaves the barrel, passes through holes in these baffles, exits the tube and heads for your target. The gases from the expansion chamber follow the bullet, are slowed by the baffles, and leave the tube with less kinetic energy than they would have if there were no baffles. Less KE means reduced recoil, no muzzle flash, and less noise. Simple as that."

Sunrise and a plan for the day. Hike up the canyon to Kate's petroglyphs, pass through her oasis in the morning, stop there in the afternoon.

David laced his boots and collected his gear. Climbing gloves and coiled rope. Holstered Browning and extra magazines. Daypack containing apples, canteen, notebook, moccasins, pocket knife, hardtack biscuits, snake bite kit. Before starting out, he wrapped his rifles in a tarp, slipped them into a shallow hole near the tent, and placed a note on the Jimmy's windshield: *If you want to die today, touch this truck.*

Above Kate's oasis, he crossed a chest-deep creek, traversed a narrow granite ledge, braved a ravine thick with brush and snakes. Higher in the canyon, he clambered across a talus slope above the creek and followed remnants of a prospector's pathway to the base of a twin waterfall. The rope ladder he and Kate had climbed be-

tween the falls was gone, leaving a 50-foot scramble over wet, fria-
ble shale and no sure way back down, but he found handholds and
balance and pulled himself up, in then out of the rushing streams.
Beyond the crest, incised on black boulders scattered among cottonwood trees, were Kate's petroglyphs. Birds, bighorn sheep, rat-
tlesnakes, coyotes, stick figures of men, and her favorite, one that
might have been a turtle.

He sat cross-legged in the shade of a cottonwood, took out his
notebook, worried the stem off an apple, waited for an idea. Why
had he come? His trek filled the day and that was all it did. He'd
expected more for his sunburn. Insight, perhaps, or closure.

Grab the daypack. Rappel alongside the two waterfalls. Leave
the rope for whoever might come next. Backtrack down the canyon, dive into the plunge pool at Kate's oasis, swim to her waterfall, stand beneath the icy cascade until you're numb. Slip into your
moccasins and walk them dry on the way to camp.

Sundown.
Alpenglow.
Campfire.
Fox and drumstick.

He was awake at first light. Where to today, if anywhere? Another canyon? Another waterfall? Maybe drive over to the hot
springs, though there would be people to deal with.

People.

They came to the desert for peace and quiet and couldn't wait to
start conversations and crowd into pools of hot water with strangers.
David told himself, "You knew how it would be," walked back to
his truck, reached in for a canteen, heard a deep, distant rumble, and
felt a jolt. Moments later a second sharp arrival rattled the Jimmy.

"Lots of shakers lately. God is angry with us. He'll send The Big One if we don't change our evil ways."

A desert rat had come up behind him, long grey ponytail, face deep-lined from years in the sun, sleeveless t-shirt: *Got Jesus? I Do! You Should!* He pointed to the license plate.

"Alaska. Long way off."

"It is."

"Praise Jesus! Where you headed?"

"Home."

"This child of God has never shared His gospel in Alaska. Might you have room for a rider?"

"No."

"You don't really mean that. The Lord knows your name, He knows you're here with me now, and He will reward you. Jesus said . . ."

"Save it. Jesus said a lot of things."

David filled his canteen at the campground pump, then drove across the valley, past sand dunes, past the salt lake, past the old salt works, to his camp. Afternoon became evening. Evening became a star-filled night, clear and cold. There would be a skin of ice on the plunge pool by midnight.

A strong tremor shook the Inyos, followed by a crashing rock-fall up-canyon. Nothing like earthquakes and the Milky Way to remind you that the mountains and the universe don't know you're here.

The fox accepted her drumstick and lay down near David to eat.

For days, from sunrise to sunset, he sat and watched the valley. After breakfast one morning he loaded his ice chests in the Jimmy and told the fox, "If you want more drumsticks, someone has to go to Bishop to get them. Besides, I'm out of coffee. Want to come along and help me do laundry? No? Okay. I'll be back tonight."

Bishop. Too many people, too much noise.

Laundromat. Firewood. Groceries and barbecued chickens. Don't forget to buy extra drumsticks. Ice. Gas. Check the tires. Stop at the post office on the way out of town, then head back to solitude and the fox. Back to where time passes but seems to stand still. Back to quiet days and campfire nights. Back to where the natural world is all a man needs.

17

Joe's Cave, June 11, 1991.

"I just started tracking Copeland's credit card transactions," Ben said. "He charged gas and groceries in Bishop a week ago and mailed a check to clear his account. Nothing since."

Joe said, "He could be back in Sitka by now."

"John Amory would let us know right away. And there'd be a trail of purchases. No, Copeland's gone to Saline Valley. I'm calling the Inyo County Sheriff."

"Know him?"

"Just his name."

When the phone rang, Sheriff Alan Davis told his dispatcher, "If that's another complaint from Betty Schultz about Morgana Jones' pet rooster, tell her I'm not in. Don't tell her I'll call back."

"It's a Sonoma County Sheriff's Deputy. Ben Hyatt. He asked for you."

"Davis here. What can I do for you, Deputy Hyatt?"

Ben detailed the case—what he and Joe knew and what they thought they knew. "I was about to put out a statewide BOLO for Copeland and his truck. It's a red 1970 Ford F-350, long bed. Alaska plates. But I think he's gone to Saline Valley."

"My backyard. Is he armed?"

"Probably."

"Dangerous?"

"I don't think he wants to hurt anyone."

"Can you be here tomorrow by 10 a.m.? I've got an airplane and I could use some seat time. We'll fly the valley, take a look around. Haven't been to the Chicken Strip for a while."

"Chicken Strip?"

"Primitive airstrip near the Saline Valley hot springs. The runway's raw dirt or loose gravel, depending on your definition. It can be a bit uneven. You land uphill, take off downhill. More and more people camp at the springs every year. Maybe someone's seen your suspect."

At the Bishop airport the next day, Sheriff Davis said, "Okay, Ben. Show me what you're packing . . . scoped AR15, Beretta 92FS, binoculars. Yeah, you're ready."

"Nice airplane."

"Bush plane. Cessna 180. Bought her in Anchorage, flew her down here, rebuilt her from prop to tail. Kept the tundra tires so I can land anywhere. Hop in."

Fifteen minutes out of Bishop, Davis said, "Down there. The road into Saline Valley. We'll follow it. We'll be over the salt lake in a short while."

"Quite a view. Mountains and valleys, valleys and mountains."

"Canyons, too. Lots of places to hide. It's Bureau of Land Management wilderness almost as far as you can see. No law enforcement for miles. People police themselves, mostly. Clothing is optional at one of the springs. For some, that's an excuse to get rowdy."

"I did my share of that."

"Good times and hangovers. Ah, there's the Chicken Strip. Hold on, we've got a crosswind . . . Okay, we're down. Smooth as butter."

At the campsites and bathing pools, Ben showed his badge and held out a photograph of David Copeland.

"Excuse me. We're looking for this person. Perhaps you've seen him?"

"Sorry to bother you. Do you recognize the man in the picture?"

"Ma'am, have you seen this fellow?"

"Sir, does he look familiar?"

"Sort of. Clean shaven, though. Shorter hair. Older, too, praise Jesus! Driving a beat up Jimmy with Alaska plates. Unfriendly. Not a follower of Jesus."

"Did you catch a name?"

"No, but this child of God figures you don't have to tell your name if you don't want to. The Lord knows who you are. Didn't say much, except that he was going home. It seemed like he has troubles, trials, and worries. He needs Jesus in his life."

"When did you talk to him?"

"Two days ago. No, three. Three days ago."

"What color was the Jimmy?"

"White."

"Okay. Thanks."

"What'd he do?"

"We just want to ask him a few questions."

Walking back to the plane Davis said, "Three days? The man and the Jimmy are long gone, Ben. Besides, you're looking for a red Ford pickup. The Alaska plates could be a coincidence."

"David Copeland's in this valley. He's got nowhere else to go."

"Well, let's get back in the air and see what we can see. We might get lucky, but if he hears us coming, he'll just crawl under a rock. No shortage of those. Ready? Bump, bump . . . and . . . we're up."

"Hey, what's that? Next to those sand dunes."

"1958 Ford station wagon. Somebody left it there brand new, in 1959. People use it for target practice."

"On the other side of the lake. Looks like tire tracks heading up a draw."

"Good eyes . . . Ah, they just end near an old dump truck and that shack. Abandoned mining claim. There's lots of them out here."

David heard the plane before he saw it. He ducked under the camouflage nets, crouched beside the truck, gripped his binoculars. What was an Alaskan bush plane doing out here? It slowed and circled low overhead, the passenger looking around, leaning out, peering down, wearing a cap that said Sheriff.

Ben said, "There's nobody down there."

"Let's go north, back toward Big Pine and Bishop. Should be easy to spot a white Jimmy on the road."

"Or off one."

That evening at Ben's motel, the manager said, "Message for you, sir."

Call John Amory in Sitka.

"Ben? Joe told me where you're staying. I saw David Copeland's truck in town and pulled it over. He wasn't driving. Turns out he swapped keys with a friend about five weeks ago. Got a pen and paper?"

Ben called Joe.

"I think Copeland's driving a white 1974 GMC K5. White fiberglass hardtop, big tires, black rims, dents, rust, Alaska plates. The vehicle was at the hot springs campground three days ago. No trace of it since."

Then he called Alan Davis.

"Maybe you're right, Ben. Maybe he is in Saline Valley. Let's fly back tomorrow and check out canyons on the west side where streams flow all year. That's where I'd camp, near water. I'm an ex-sniper, like Copeland, so I'd also be thinking about concealment."

"His girlfriend mentioned a waterfall."

"Well, there's quite a few."

"I'd like to take another look at that shack and the dump truck."

"Good idea. See you in the a.m."

Bush plane, flying south, flying high. Best to keep binoculars, a rifle, and some ammunition handy and stay near the camo nets. David heard the plane several times, but it didn't come over until mid-afternoon, flying low, flying slow. Same passenger, same hat. Was that a rifle barrel in the window?

"Anything, Ben?"

"Don't know. Let's hit it once more."

"If there's someone there and he thinks we've left, he might show himself. So we'll make like we've gone home. Then we'll pop back. Lock and load."

The bush plane again. Smart move. He hadn't expected another visit. David ran, M14 in one hand, a box of cartridges in the other, camouflage nets too far, miner's shack too far, the dump truck his only hope. Wedged under the driveline, he held his breath against the smells of old motor oil and dead mice. The plane flew overhead, loud and close. A ground-level pass followed, leaving a prop-wash sandstorm. It didn't come back. Three feet away, a rattlesnake—tail buzzing, tongue tasting the air—became a tight coil. David said, "Don't. Please. Don't." He rolled away from the steady rattle saying, "Calm down. I'm leaving. It's all yours."

"Still nothing," Ben said, "but I'd bet he's down there watching us."

"The only way to find out is to go in on the ground."

"Well, that is something to think about."

"I don't have an army to throw at this, just three deputies and a couple of 4x4s."

———————

Twilight.

Campfire.

Maybe the passenger's binoculars didn't mean anything and maybe that wasn't a rifle barrel. He hadn't seen official markings on the plane. Maybe the hat just *said* Sheriff. Probably nothing to worry about. No one knew he was out here. Time to turn in. He could rest easy.

A sharp bark at the tent door woke David from a dream of Kate and Molly. The fox ran off, then barked a distant alarm from the darkness.

Get out of the sleeping bag fast. Jeans, shirt, moccasins. Unwrap the M14. Raise the rifle and sight through the scope. Two sets of headlights lit the jeep track. Were there also men on foot, flanking his camp? The vehicles stopped and idled, one behind the other. Then, breaking glass, bottles thrown against rocks, boombox music, spotlights. "Over there! Coyote!" The shooters drank and argued for a few minutes. Firing bursts into the air, they drove down to the main road and into the night. David began to shiver. He hadn't realized how cold it was. The fox ran back and forth through the camp before she curled up next to him in the tent. "It's okay now," David said. "It's okay"

Soft light of dawn.
The unyielding glare of midday.
Sundown.
Night.
Campfire.

David relived his time at 805 Grove Street, the crossroad of four lives. Maybe Ed had been right, maybe they should have quit school for the money. In a year or two he could have returned to the quiet academic career he'd always wanted—with Kate or without her—and the world would have left him alone. Life was pretty much a solo act right from the start anyway. He should have paid more attention to Kate. Ian would have never touched her if he'd just stayed home.

Let go of the past.

He turned from the fire and looked up at the stars. There'd be a new moon tomorrow night and a new day after that. Then what?

He slept late, well past sunrise. The fox lay inside the tent door, eyes open, waiting. Coffee and hardtack for him, drumstick for her. A cold-water swim. Sit for hours, listen to nature's silence, doze in the warming air. Another dip in the plunge pool. Stand once more under the waterfall.

At noon there were two small earthquakes. Hot afternoon winds blew dust devils across the valley floor, then the late-day shadow of the Inyos slid east and brought a chill to the camp.

Night.
Campfire.
David held out a drumstick and said, "That's all, girl. You've been a good friend."

He sat in the Jimmy looking over his collection of photographs, wrote a short letter to Kate, stacked the last of his wood in the fire ring, looked again through the photos and chose five.

Annie and the boys.

Roommates on the porch at 805 Grove Street.

Grunt brothers in Vietnam, David Copeland and Glenn Siegel.

Molly.

Kate.

One by one he draped the pictures over a glowing log and watched them curl to ash.

Let go of the past.

If you can.

——— ———

Two days later.

"Thin air, Joe," Ben said. "Thin air."

"They're always somewhere. You did your best and it was pretty good in my book. You taught me a few things. But you know, it's kind of funny."

"What is?"

"My last case. It goes cold."

18

Three years later.

Captain Ben Hyatt was in the habit of answering his phone right away. You never knew what might come in—an emergency, a routine matter, a tip on a new case or information that might warm up a cold one. He took the first call of the day.

"*Captain?* Congratulations. It's Alan Davis, Ben. We've located the individual you were looking for in Saline Valley."

"When can I talk to him?"

"I guess I should have said that we've identified his skeletal remains. Near the miner's shack and the dump truck. I've got a deputy sitting out there, but I need him in the office, so I'm flying over tomorrow to button things up. Want to come along? Helicopter this time. We'll set down near the shack."

"Did he leave any firearms?"

"An M14, which he could have used on us. I doubt it's ever been fired. A Browning Hi-Power, which he used on himself. There's a suppressor, but it's not attached. Also a strange little thing that looks homemade."

"De Lisle."

"De-what?"

"I'll explain. Any ammunition?"

"One box each, 9mm and .45 ACP. Two boxes 7.62x51mm NATO."

"Thanks, Alan. I'll see you in the morning."

At David's camp the next day, Ben asked, "Who called it in?"

"A geologist with a mining company. He noticed the Jimmy and the tent under the camouflage nets, walked toward them, and almost tripped over the rib cage. He had the good sense not to touch anything."

"We flew right over Copeland."

"Two or three times."

"I'll bet he made us the first day. But there was no sign of him."

"He did what a sniper does. Covered his tracks. Didn't leave a footprint or a scrap of paper, not even ash from his campfire. We would never have seen him."

"The man wanted to be alone."

"He left a note on the dashboard." *To whoever finds me, my apologies. Everyone has to die somewhere.* "And a sealed envelope on the driver's seat." *For Kate Anderson, Port Angeles, Washington. Last Will and Testament of David Michael Copeland.* "There's another sealed envelope. It's also for her."

"I'll see that she gets them."

"We found a dead Kit fox curled up next to a sleeping bag inside the tent. What's left of Copeland is in front of the Jimmy. Coyotes got him."

"He knew they would."

"Single bullet hole in the right temple, pistol three feet away on the ground. Looks like a suicide."

"Yes. It does."

"Damn shame."

"Yeah . . . I'm going to wander up the hill."

"Watch out for snakes."

Ben stood at Kate's oasis for a few minutes. She and David Copeland had been young and innocent when they came here. He imagined them in the plunge pool, lovers full of life and promise, laughing, carefree. Like she'd said, kids in the desert. He turned and walked back to their fire ring.

"What's up there, Ben?"

"Waterfall. Swimming hole. What are you going to do about the Jimmy?"

"We'll winch it down to the main road. Then a flatbed wrecker can haul it to our impound yard. You take the guns."

———

Kate Anderson opened her front door before Ben knocked.

"You found David."

"I'm sorry, Ms. Anderson. Someone else did, the week before last."

"How did . . .?"

"He took his own life. We think it was three years ago."

"Oh . . . Come in. Where?"

"Saline Valley, at your old campsite. He left these envelopes for you. No one's opened them."

"Oh . . . Thank you. I was just thinking about him. I think about him all the time. Did he really kill Ian and Edward?"

"He did."

"When David was here I told him about Ian and the abortion. And Edward . . . the songs . . . that's why . . . both of them."

"It looks that way."

She took a photograph from the mantel—Saline Valley at sunset. "I thought there was nothing out there. I was wrong. It's wonderful. You feel small but not in a bad way. You feel . . . free."

"Ms. Anderson . . ."

"Kate."

"Kate. Did David contact you after he went to California?"

"Once. He sent a short letter. It came a few days after you and your partner were here."

Without my notebooks, the attorney says, there's no proof I wrote the songs and no point in contesting Ed's copyrights. I don't know where the notebooks are or if they still exist. I'll stop by in a few days. I'll call first. Give Mitch a pat on the head for me.

"I knew something had happened when he didn't call."

"His will . . . I'd like to know what it says, but it's okay if you don't want to tell me. Nothing official, I'm just curious."

"Um . . . Mr. Hyatt?"

"Ben."

"Ben. Would you like a cup of coffee? Or tea?"

"Coffee if it's no trouble."

"No trouble at all. It'll be nice to make coffee for someone besides myself."

Ben heard her crying in the kitchen.

She brought a tray, tried to smile, and said, "Coffee cake, too. Homemade."

"Thank you, Kate."

"You came here to give me David's letters. You could have mailed them."

"I didn't want them to just show up. They seemed more important than that."

"You're very kind. Ben . . . do you . . . do you ever go back through your life and regret your mistakes?"

"I do. I think everyone does, because, I suppose, there's no getting away from them. Sometimes, I need to remind myself that I can't change things that happened, I can't make things happen that didn't, I can't take back words I've said, I can't say what I should have said."

"You make it sound easy."

"It's never easy, but there's not much else you can do. You have to go on living."

"David and I didn't just break up. I was in bed with a drug dealer one night when he got home. David walked out. He never would have quit school and gone to Alaska if it wasn't for me. It's all my fault. I'll never be able to change that."

"We all make mistakes. Don't blame yourself. You were young."

"My God! I could have caught syphilis or something else. I could have made David sick. And my son . . ."

"But that didn't happen, Kate."

"No . . . No, it didn't."

"I'm flying home tomorrow evening. Call if you want to talk. I'll be at this number."

She called early the next morning.

"Can you come over, Ben? I found something. I'll be in the barn. I made coffee."

"David had this crate in his room when we met. I never looked inside, never saw him open it. I took everything out this morning, books, clothing, maps, his old camera, this photograph of the four of us on the porch at 805 Grove Street, and David's flannel shirts. I used to wear them. This was my favorite. I unfolded it to put it on and his notebooks fell out. His songs are all here. And there were two cassette tapes. One says, 'New Songs.' The other says, 'For Josh and Toby.'"

"What's on them?"

"I don't know. I'll have to buy a tape player."

"What's that little wire loop?"

"I didn't even notice it."

Ben tugged on the loop and lifted the floor of the crate up and out. An empty wooden box labeled De Lisle Carbine .45 ACP filled most of the space. A cookie tin held Captain Michael Davidson Copeland's medals and commando beret, his notes on De Lisles, and a tattered booklet: *Pistolet Automatique Browning, Modele 1935, Calibre 9mm.*

"David's father's guns," Ben said. "We knew he hid them somewhere to bring them into the country. This is where they were."

"The guns David used to kill Ian and Edward?"

"Yes."

"I opened both envelopes last night. This was in the first one."

People die. Life goes on. The mountains don't know we're here.

"Here's David's will."

Having no surviving relatives, I, David Michael Copeland, give Kate Alice Anderson the entirety of my estate. 1) My house and land in Sitka, Alaska. 2) All my other material possessions. 3) My intellectual property and all rights thereto.

"I don't deserve any of it."

"David wouldn't agree."

"He could have proved he'd written the songs. He didn't have to . . ."

"The songs are yours now. He'd want that."

"I think about him all the time, Ben. I can't stop thinking about him. I know what I threw away."

"Do you want me to send his remains?"

"No . . . No . . . I . . . Yes. I'll make sure he's with his wife and children."

She looked at the photograph again, touched the image, said, "Grove Street," and whispered, "David."

———————

The telephone woke Joe D'Alessandro from his afternoon nap. It didn't ring much these days. He said, "I'll get it, Rose."

"Joe. It's Ben. How's my old friend?"

"Your old friend is retired and bored. Your old friend's wife says he should get out more."

"We'll talk about that in a minute. I have a plan. The other reason I called is, they found David Copeland's bones in Saline Valley."

"Where you said he'd be."

"I went to see Kate Anderson and gave her a couple of letters he wanted her to have. We talked."

"You've got a good heart, Ben."

"And I found out how Copeland's father brought the Hi-Power and the De Lisle into the U.S. We can't do anything until the British Government decides if the guns are still their property, so we're holding on to them for the time being."

"Come for dinner. Lasagna, Chianti, cannoli. Rose would love to see you. We'll celebrate your promotion. Got your own Cave, they tell me. You can stay overnight. Hey, bring the De Lisle. I'd like to take a look at it."

"I'll tell you the whole story. Sad case."

"Every case is sad, Ben. There aren't many happy endings in our line of work. Now, what's this about a plan?"

"You said that you like to fish. There's a trout-filled lake I've heard about on the east side of the Sierras and a cabin and a boat Alan Davis says we can use."

"So?"

"So I stay over. We get up early and head out. We eat breakfast at a roadside diner I know, no disrespect to Rose and her cooking. We pick up bait and supplies in Bishop. We find the lake and the cabin."

"Then what?"

"We fish for a week, maybe two."

"I'm listening."

AUTHOR'S NOTE

I first learned of William Godfrey De Lisle's carbine while browsing away a rainy afternoon at Powell's Books in Portland, Oregon. I had been looking into suppressed firearms to flesh out ideas that would become *On Grove Street*. For a handgun, the Belgian Browning Hi-Power was a no-brainer. But a center-fire rifle with a thread-on suppressor wouldn't be quiet enough for what I had in mind and it would be too obvious—there'd be no mystery and no story.

At Powell's, I looked, by chance, through a copy of *Combat Guns and Infantry Weapons* (Airlife Publishing Ltd, Shrewsbury, England, 1996) and found an obscure firearm with an interesting, equally obscure history: the De Lisle Commando Carbine. An on-line search led to Wikipedia, Google Images, many—too many to mention—good sources, and Ian Skennerton's masterful, authoritative pamphlet, *Special Service Lee-Enfields . . . Commando & Auto Models*, available at skennerton.com.

To see a replica De Lisle in operation—originals are few and far between—you can do no better than to watch YouTube > Military Arms Channel > De Lisle Carbine. You will hear that there is very little to hear when a De Lisle is fired.

There's a first-rate video of the Browning Hi-Power—fired and field-stripped, lore and history—at YouTube > Military Arms Channel > Browning Hi-Power.

"Bren Gun" in Captain Copeland's war diary (Chapter 14) refers to the Bren light machine gun. Explore Google Images and search "Bren light machine gun Wikipedia."

Curious about Mt. Edgecumbe? Search "Mount Edgecumbe AK" at Google Images. Or visit the Hathi Trust Digital Library online, where *The Mount Edgecumbe Volcanic Field—A Geologic History* by J. R. Riehle loads slowly at times but is worth the wait.

Made in the USA
Columbia, SC
15 November 2024

46312614R00086